BENTO

SECRET GROWTH

ISBN-10: 1466338911
EAN-13: 9781466338913
Library of Congress Control Number: 2011916797

CreateSpace, North Charleston, SC

The dominant primordial beast was strong in Buck, and under the fierce condition of trail life it grew and grew. Yet it was a secret growth. His newborn cunning gave him poise and control.

Jack London
The Call of the Wild

1

I was sitting on the couch wearing only my underwear when the Boston police pounded on my apartment door. *Bang, bang, bang!* "Arnold Humphrey! We have a court order commanding you to leave the premises. If you do not answer this door, we will break it down. Do the easy thing and open the door."

This shouldn't have been a revelation. I had seen the eviction notices posted on my door, and I had ignored them. My landlord had regularly called for the past three months, and I had ignored him too. When the police came, I thought all I needed to do was ignore them as well, and they would eventually leave. My entire strategy was to pretend everything was normal.

I got a jolt of reality when the police broke my door down. One of the officers yanked me off the couch and pushed me into the middle of the room. "Are you crazy? No wonder you're broke. In your apartment in the middle of the day only wearing your underwear. Now go put on some clothes. And whatever you leave, you're not getting back."

As I dressed, the four policemen checked around my nearly empty apartment to see if anyone else was there. Anything of worth like compact discs, a television, or stereo equipment had long been hocked. The only items I treasured were my computer and the pages of my manuscript. I had spent my last three months working feverishly on an exposé about the World Trade Center attack.

The manuscript was the only thing I grabbed. Since my computer was a desktop, I couldn't bring it. I had nowhere to store everything, and no money for self-storage. I couldn't count on my parents either. I had burned that bridge when I cashed my college tuition checks for two years without attending a single class. I lived the college life without really being in college.

During those days I came into contact with some conspiracy theorists who made me hot on the World Trade Center bombings. I knew many of the theories were farfetched since I had watched the planes hit the World Trade Center on TV. Then again, if magician David Copperfield could make the Statue of Liberty disappear, the U.S. government could certainly fudge some photographs.

I manically wrote pages demanding that Bush be taken in front of The Hague for war crimes. I documented how a U.S.-supported Pakistani government was harboring bin Laden. I had written over three hundred pages and was convinced that I was going to be rich and famous. Nobel Peace Prize winner. President of the United States.

Reality kicked in again when I found myself standing on the sidewalk with only my manuscript in my hand and the clothes on my back. I needed to go somewhere, but in the last six months I had alienated myself from my friends. Never mind; I didn't have a cell phone anyway. Forced to make an immediate decision about my future, I used the remainder of my money on a bus ticket to New York City, where I hoped to promote my book.

When I arrived in New York for the first time in my life, I didn't have a clue where to find publishing houses. Still optimistic, I hoped to sign a contract with an editor within hours and receive an advance, which I could use to rent an apartment. Even as I huddled in a tunnel in Central Park during a storm and rummaged through a trashcan for food, I was sure I would soon realize my dream of getting published. But when I finally located a literary agency, I was escorted out of the building and threatened by the police with vagrancy.

I roamed the streets of Manhattan alone, penniless, and exhausted. The one thing I never expected about being homeless was how hard it was to find a place to sit down. In three days I had been kicked out of no less than ten McDonald's franchises, Grand Central Terminal, Penn Station, and the Port Authority. I hadn't slept more than fifteen minutes straight since arriving in New York, and I began to believe the CIA was following me because of my knowledge about the World Trade Center attack and the Bush cover-up.

Finally, I was so beaten down I had to do something. I had to sleep. I had to get off my feet. I had never lived lavishly, but I had also never been reduced to such a meager existence. I was desperate. But where could I go and whom could I trust to help me? My knowledge was too dangerous to the United States' national security. If I was caught, I would be waterboarded. If I survived that, they would pull out my fingernails. If I beat that as well, my head would be placed in a vise and squished until my brain squirted out of my ears.

But then my mind would shift, and I saw myself as a hero for uncovering Bush's crimes. I imagined my picture on the front page of every major magazine and newspaper in the country. If

I made the right decisions and won, then I would get everything I wanted, and I wanted to spin the world on my middle finger like a basketball.

And then I came up with an idea. The plan was genius. Just like I was uncovering the hoax of the World Trade Center attack, I was calling the bluff of the people following me. *You people think you're so smart. Try this on for size.* I would show the world who was calling the shots. At the corner of Thirty-third Street and First Avenue, I laid down my manuscript and stripped off my shirt, pants, underwear, and socks.

Now that I was naked, the September air chilled my body, the cold only combatted by the sheer ecstasy pumping through my veins. This was perfect. Finally free from the constraints of society, I marched down the street with only my manuscript in hand, convinced that I was about to be crowned king of the world. I imagined a white limousine pulling up and me jumping in with George W. sitting in the back saying in his Texas twang, "All right, fella. You're too smart for us. You win. What do you want?"

But alas, the plan didn't go so well. Instead a cop yelled, "What are you doing? You're naked!"

Though I heard the mockery in his voice, I sprinted down the street, the tiny pebbles pricking my bare feet, until another policeman came out of nowhere and tackled me to the ground. Now on top of me, he tried to pin me down. "Where do you think you're going with no clothes on?" he asked.

It is an uncomfortable feeling when the emperor suddenly realizes he's wearing no clothes. "I don't know," I replied.

"Are you all right, son?"

I closed my eyes and shook my head, so scared I was about to cry.

The policeman's grip softened. "Are you cool? No problem? Can I let you up?"

"I'm fine." The officer pulled me to my feet. I was shocked by his kindness.

"It's all right. We'll get you inside. Everything is going to be okay."

The policeman stood there a moment in the frigid air, apparently trying to decide what to do next. People were starting to gather, and I heard laughter. Another officer came over and looked at my privates and laughed.

Immediately, I moved my hands to cover myself in my first act of decency in a while. Luckily the arresting officer took pity and escorted me over to the police car and opened the door. "It's too cold to be outside with no cover. You'll be fine in here for now."

"Thank you," I muttered.

"Where are your clothes?"

"Down the street a block or two."

"I'll go get them."

I dropped my head, believing this was my punishment. They were going to drag me to Guantanamo Bay, where my only human contact would be from my torturers.

A few minutes later the policeman opened the car door. "Here's your clothes. Put them on. We're going to take you somewhere safe."

"Jail?"

"No. Not jail. We're taking you to a hospital. They can help someone like you much better than we can."

I took a deep breath and relaxed. I needed to concentrate on passing my next test. *Are they taking me to the hospital for psychological testing? Medical induced torture?*

I immediately thought of Kafka's *The Trial*, which I had recently read. In it, a person is on trial but does not know his crime. The premise was spooky enough that I thought of that book several times a day. Every time something out of the ordinary was thrust up on me and my mettle was tested, I would think of *The Trial*.

I didn't get to this point overnight. There had been buildup over the last few years beginning my freshman year of college. My first semester at Boston University, I lost five thousand dollars gambling on football. I had no choice but to dip into my school money. I tried to win it back so I could repay my parents, but instead I fell deeper into the hole. It ended when my parents insisted on seeing my report card.

They cut me off, and I hadn't spoken to them since. I lived in the same apartment the last three years, barely able to hold on to it as long as I did by supporting myself with an array of jobs ranging from manual labor to retail sales. Before that I drank a lot of beer. Surfed the Internet. Read a lot of books. For someone who was not attending school, I read a lot of books. There would be days when I would sit on my couch all day and read, breaking only for meals. That's how my mind worked. I'd get something in my head, and I would not drop it until I exhausted the idea.

"What were you thinking, getting naked in the middle of the street?" asked the officer.

I didn't answer, not because I was angry, but because there was no way I could explain what was going on in my head. Luckily it was a short drive to the hospital. I wasn't in handcuffs as the officer and his partner escorted me to the waiting room. Since I had a cop on either side, everyone turned and looked at me with accusing eyes.

"You can take a seat if you promise not to cause trouble," said the officer on my right.

I looked around at the strange faces. "I don't like it. Everyone is staring at me."

"I know you're scared, but everything is going to be OK. They're going to help you."

While the policemen spoke to the receptionist, I stood up and paced the emergency room with my head down and my hands behind my back. I believed the doctors and nurses were all CIA and they were all trying to figure out how much I knew and what danger I presented to the United States government. Everyone was acting like they worked at the hospital. Their job was to make me believe I was in a real hospital. They had brought me to be analyzed by the best and brightest to see what I knew.

The policemen returned with a man wearing a white coat and spectacles that gave him a scholarly look. On closer inspection I noticed the doctor's eyebrows connected and realized this quack was no scholar. He was just some worm embarrassed about his unibrow and wearing glasses to hide it.

"Hi. I'm Dr. Rider. I understand you're hearing voices."

I looked at the doctor sideways and then at the cops. I needed to be very careful about what I said. I didn't want to be caught in double-talk. I felt like the best thing to do was be totally honest. "I didn't say I was hearing voices. Good God! Who told you I was hearing voices?"

"All right, Mr. Humphrey. Calm down. What seems to be the problem? I was under the impression you thought you were hearing voices or being followed."

I looked over my shoulder. "You see how people are watching me. Everyone is watching me."

"This is what he's been saying all along," said one policeman.

"I'll take it from here, officers. Thank you very much."

The officers walked away without another word. Dr. Rider licked his lips and looked over my shoulder. "Why do you think people are watching you? I don't see anything out of the ordinary."

I couldn't tell if the doctor was being concerned or condescending, but either way I didn't feel comfortable. I started to walk away. "This is a big mistake. I don't belong in here. I just need a place to sleep."

The doctor placed his hand on my shoulder. "Relax. Take a deep breath and relax. You're in a safe place now."

I looked up and mustered a slight smile. *Is he trying to hurt me or help me?* My mind swung back and forth like a pendulum; I couldn't make up my mind.

"And don't worry. We'll take care of you. Let's get you to the mental health emergency room. We'll give you something to eat. For hospital food it's actually not bad."

"Mental health unit? This is getting absurd. I'm no nut."

"Do you want to be in a quiet place where you can sleep or not? Because I don't know what you expected, but this is not a hotel. It's a hospital, and I can assure you no one will follow you in there."

"You're not going to keep me there forever, are you?"

The doctor smiled. "I promise we won't keep you here forever. You can ease your mind of that."

The doctor held the door and led me through the main emergency room, where we were greeted by beeping heart monitors and orderlies pushing rattling gurneys. Doctors and nurses were running in every direction. No one even noticed Dr. Rider or me walking through the eye of this human hurricane.

At the other end of the room, once again Dr. Rider held the door. It was decidedly calmer on the other side. No one was hustling around. Patients in light blue gowns were scattered across a large room. Some paced just as I had earlier. Others sat in chairs and spoke to one another. Behind the counter in the middle of the room sat two young nurses in navy blue scrubs, so enthralled by their computers that they just glanced at us when we entered the room.

Surrounding this room were four private rooms with a single hospital bed in each. Dr. Rider led me to one of these and patted the bed. "I have to leave now, but the nurses will be with you shortly. I'll be back later, and we'll see how we can help you. And don't worry," the doctor said with a smile. "You're in good hands. Take it easy. We'll help you feel better. I promise."

Finally alone, I leaned back on the bed, hoping to get some much needed sleep, when a patient walked into my room with a newspaper in his hand. He was a stout man with a pug nose, jagged torn-up teeth, and rampant acne.

"Do you want to read the newspaper?" he asked.

I snatched the paper out of his hand. "Let me see that," I declared. Maybe my name was in the newspaper. Maybe my arrival had been announced. My mind continued to course through rapid cycles between Utopia and hell.

I began to flip through the pages, but after a minute, I was so exhausted I couldn't concentrate. "That's all right," I said, handing back the paper. "I think I'm just going to try and catch some shut-eye."

"What's that?"

"Sleep. I need some sleep. Do you understand sleep?"

"That's funny. I just woke up." He smiled, showing those horrendous teeth. "Are you going to take a nap?"

I raised my finger to my mouth. "Shh."

"Oh. I see. You don't want to make friends. You want to do it all alone. I know your kind. Think you're smarter than everyone else."

As the man walked away, I shook my head in disgust, leaned back on the gurney, and tried to sleep, but before I even had a chance to close my eyes, a nurse walked up.

"I'm Elaine. I'm one of the nurses in the ER. I'm going to take your blood pressure, if that's all right."

"Why won't everyone just leave me alone?" I cried out. Then I understood. They were going to torture me with sleep deprivation.

"Please calm down, Mr. Humphrey."

"I need to sleep. Doesn't anyone understand that? All I need is some sleep, and then I'll go on my merry way. No questions asked. No answers questioned."

"Excuse me, Mr. Humphrey. But you were found walking down the street with no clothes on just a half hour ago. That is not normal behavior. We need to find out why you did that."

"Uhhh!"

"Are you having a bad day, Mr. Humphrey?"

"Try a bad year."

"I'm sorry. It'll get better." Elaine wrapped the black Velcro around my left arm, placed the stethoscope on the inside of my elbow, and began pumping. The black wrap tightened around my arm until she released the air. I felt my heart pulsing inside my arm.

"One sixty over one hundred. A little high. Now I need to check your heart rate." Elaine grabbed my wrist and looked down at her watch as she counted the beats. "Eighty-two. A little high as well, but it's understandable in your condition."

"What do you mean, in my condition?"

"I'm talking about your state of agitation. Now I need to get your height and weight. So if you could follow me, we'll get that out of the way."

Elaine picked up her manila folder, and without looking back, she led me to the corner of the room where there was a scale.

"First, we'll check your height."

I turned around to measure myself.

"Five ten," said Elaine.

"I know."

"You'd be surprised how many people don't know how tall they are. Now turn around, and I'll check your weight." Elaine pushed the lever back and forth until it balanced at 160 pounds.

"Now I need to get a urine sample, so if you could go urinate in this cup and bring it back to me, that would be great."

"I don't know if I can go to the bathroom. I haven't drunk anything in a while."

"We've got time. If you want, you can drink from the pitcher of water sitting on the counter. That's what it's there for. Anyway, keep the cup and bring the urine sample to the nurse's station when you're ready."

I didn't take a bathroom break or drink a cup of water. Instead, I marched straight to my bed and lay down without bothering to pull down the sheets. This was as close to heaven as I had been in a long time.

2

I slept soundly on my back, which I never did except when the tank was completely empty, and there was no doubt I had been running on fumes for the past couple of days. When I awoke later, I was starving. Orderlies had just delivered food, and the smells drove me crazy. Roast beef, brown rice, broccoli, milk, coffee, a slice of bread, and applesauce for dessert. The patients sat in chairs with the trays in their laps. There was some griping about the food, but I wasn't complaining. At least it was a well-balanced meal.

I thought of Mom's meatloaf at Sunday dinner with my grandparents. It had been a tradition as long as I could remember. I wondered what my parents told them. I supposed I could call my grandparents. Surely they would have a soft spot. But I didn't want to do that. Though I may have been struggling these last few months after a childhood that wasn't sparkling either, I was living my life on my own terms, and I was proud of that.

But my demons were never far. When I picked up my fork to dig in, I caught the food deliveryman looking at me out of the corner of his eye. Just like that, I was back on the defense. I was sure the man was trying to poison me. Even though I had not eaten for two days, I picked up my tray, put it on the floor, and leaned back in my chair.

The nurse came to me again and said, "If you're finished eating, I need your urine sample."

On the bathroom door a sign read, PLEASE DON'T CLOSE THE DOOR WHEN YOU EXIT. IT AUTOMATICALLY LOCKS.

After filling the cup and flushing the toilet, I walked out, forgetting to leave the door open. I heard the lock click behind me, followed by the voice of the uniformed security guard. "Don't close the door!"

"Sorry."

Keys jangling in his hand, he stomped over to the bathroom door. *Like he has so many other important things to do.* I thought this had to be the only job in the world more boring than handing out flyers on street corners.

Dr. Rider entered the ward. For the next hour, the patients accosted him with questions and demands. He was courteous but brief as he walked around the room, the others following him like autograph seekers sucking blood off a celebrity. Finally, Dr. Rider made it over to me.

"How are you managing?" he asked.

"Not good."

"Have you ever been in a psychiatric ward before?"

"No."

Dr. Rider paused for a moment. He seemed surprised. "How old are you, Mr. Humphrey?"

"Twenty-three."

"If you've never been to a place like this before, you must be pretty overwhelmed."

"I've been better."

"Are you still hearing voices?"

"Who said I was hearing voices? I'm not hearing voices."

"But you said people were talking about you. Is that normal for you?"

"It is when it's true."

"Do they scare you?"

"It would scare anyone. At least anyone who's sane. Who wants strangers talking about them?"

"Have you ever thought strangers were talking about you before?"

"Yes."

"But you've been able to deal with them in the past?"

"It's worse this time."

Dr. Rider paused and looked down at me with a smile. "What do you do for a living, Mr. Humphrey?"

"I don't have a job."

"How do you support yourself?"

"I don't."

"You must have had a job at some point."

"I've worked in retail off and on for the last two years."

"Why not now?"

"I got fired."

"I see. Where do you live?"

"I live on the streets."

Dr. Rider took off his glasses and wiped the lenses with a Kleenex. "I'm sorry to hear that. I didn't realize. How long have you lived on the streets?"

"Three days."

"Where did you live before you were homeless?"

"Boston."

"What brought you to New York?"

"I'm working on a book."

Dr. Rider brought his hand to his chin and began massaging it with his fingers. "Yes. I see the manuscript next to you. That's very interesting. What is it about?"

"About the government cover-up for what really happened on 9/11."

"What really happened?"

"George Bush was scared he was going to be caught for election tampering, and he needed something to divert the nation's attention. He ordered the World Trade Center bombing so his original crimes would be overlooked. I'm not saying Bush planned it. He's not that smart, but he did give the go-ahead. George W. was friends with Osama. That's a fact. There are pictures to prove that. He was buddies with their whole damn family."

Dr. Rider smiled. "I see that you are very passionate in your belief."

"You don't believe me either?" My eyes darted around the room to see who was listening. I wanted to be heard. I wanted people to know the truth.

"No, I'm not saying that. I find what you're saying very interesting. I only wonder when you started believing this."

"About a year ago. And I'm not the only one. There are a million different sites about it on the Internet."

"Is that when people started talking about you?"

"Maybe."

"Have you ever taken any psychiatric medication? Would you be open to taking medication?"

"I'm not crazy. I don't need medication. I just need a place to sleep."

"Mr. Humphrey. We offer a more comprehensive treatment plan than just providing shelter."

"Shelter is all I need."

"You were walking down the street with no clothes on. You tell me, Mr. Humphrey. Does that sound normal to you?"

"Well. I'm wearing clothes now."

"Let's strike a bargain. If you agree to medical treatment, I can assure you that you will have all the time in the world to catch up on your sleep and write your book. Is that a deal?"

"I'll try it for a little while."

Dr. Rider placed his hand on my shoulder. "That's good. That's very good."

"If there is something wrong with me, then what is it?"

"It's a little too early to say."

"But what do you think?"

"Like I said, it's a little too early to say. Sometimes the best way to tell what's wrong with a person is by what medications work for them. Do you have any other medical conditions?"

"I don't think so."

"Diabetes?"

"I don't think so."

"When was the last time you saw a doctor?"

"It's been a long time."

"On any account, we'll do some blood work to be certain. In the meantime we'll start you on Haldol."

"What is it?"

"An antipsychotic. It should help with the paranoia."

"I'm not being paranoid."

"Of course not. It will help you relax so you can sleep. I'll come by and see how you're doing later."

I was uneasy about taking medication. Like everything else, I was suspicious. I didn't know what kind of effect psychiatric medicine would have on me, and I worried the side effects would alter my judgment so that I would say or do something I normally wouldn't. So when the nurse handed over two Dixie cups, one filled with water and the other holding a single pink pill, I hesitated before throwing my head back and swallowing them both down.

"That's good, Mr. Humphrey. You should start feeling better soon," said the nurse.

That evening two staff workers came down to the emergency room to escort me into longer-term care. With a man on each elbow, I slowly walked through the hallways, stumbling over my feet since they had confiscated my shoelaces and holding my jeans up with one hand since they had also taken my belt. Inside I laughed at my predicament. Even I had the common sense to know that if I wasn't crazy, I was certainly making a good impersonation.

Still, I was looking for an opportunity to sprint for an exit and out to freedom. But there was no chance. Before every door one of the staff members would stop, find another key from his collection of many, and unlock the door, and then the three of us would advance to the other side. Finally, we arrived in front of the unit.

Fortunately the ward was probably ten times the size of the emergency room. It had a recreation room with Ping-Pong and pool tables on the left, and offices for the psychiatrists on the right. Farther up was the nurses' station with three women sitting behind glass. Two patients stood there arguing about who was a better wrestler, Hulk Hogan or Ric Flair.

"Who do we have here?" asked a staff member.

The escort looked down at the piece of paper he was holding. "It says here, Juanita, that we have an Arnold Humphrey."

"Well. Mr. Humphrey, let's get you checked in."

The mundane questioning lasted at least another half hour. Juanita asked the same questions I was asked in the emergency room. Perhaps they were checking my story? Making sure I was saying the same things? Telling the truth? Surely this wasn't such a bureaucracy that they couldn't pass along personal information to the next person and avoid all this bullshit.

When the interview was completed, Juanita stood up and placed the folder on the metal table beside her. "Thank you very much, Mr. Humphrey. I'll give you your toiletries now, and then I'll find someone to take you down to your room."

I was being run in circles and felt like a baton in a relay race, but at the same time I was relieved. I didn't know if it was from the medicine or the chance to catch some more sleep finally, but I was feeling slightly better. My shoulders felt relaxed, and I had stopped grinding my teeth. Not to mention I was being treated well. Very well. Like a baby, in fact.

A moment later a pot-bellied man, probably in his fifties, with horn-rimmed glasses waddled over with his toes pointed outward. With the crazed look in his eye, he could have been mistaken for a patient except for his identification hanging from his neck. He was dressed in a blue-and-white striped button-down, navy blue pants, and blinding white tennis shoes. In fact just about everything in the ward was white. White walls. White tiles. Nurses dressed in white. And when we reached the room at the end of the hall, the bedsheets were white as well.

"Your bunk is in the corner."

The pot-bellied man walked over to the closet and opened it to make sure the previous patient had emptied everything out, not caring that he was making a horrible racket. Or even worse, maybe he was trying to, but the three sleeping patients in the room were so comatose they didn't budge.

"Looks like everything is clean. Don't bring food in here. Food stays in the dining room. We've got a little bit of a mouse problem, so try to keep your area neat. Do I make myself clear?"

"Yeah."

"Okay. Good. Do you have any questions?"

Slowly coming to terms with reality, I looked around the dark room and then sat down on the edge of my bed. If you could call it a bed. It was more like a giant sponge wrapped in a vinyl shell. It wasn't home, but it wasn't jail either, and it certainly beat slumming under a bridge. As if the person sleeping next to me could read what I was thinking, his voice called out:

"Welcome to Shangri-la."

I squinted, but with the lights out, I could only see a black man's silhouette.

"Ever been here before?" he asked.

"Can't say that I have."

The man chuckled. "Are you crazy?"

"I hope not."

He stood up and walked over to the bathroom. He didn't bother to shut the door, and I could hear the steady stream of his whiz before the sound of the toilet flushing, which was followed by him washing his hands in the sink. He emerged from the bathroom wiping his hands with a brown paper towel before throwing it in the trash.

"Is this your first time?" I asked.

"My first time? No-o, I've been coming here off and on for years. Everyone here knows me. I practically earn frequent flyer miles, I've been here so often."

"What's your diagnosis?"

"My diagnosis? Let's see here. Well, for starters, I'm a crackhead."

"Do they know that?"

"Who?"

"The doctors."

"Of course they do. I've told them the truth. I'm in *re*-covery," he said with emphasis on the first syllable.

"Getting any better?"

"Don't care. How long were you in the ER?"

"I don't know. Four or five hours."

"That's it?"

"Yeah, why?"

"Weather's getting cold. Us crackheads gotta find a warm place to sleep. We come here in droves in the wintertime."

I had never considered that someone would want to be in a mental hospital.

"Name's Wade."

"I go by Humphrey."

In the light from the bathroom, I could see Wade more clearly. He was dark, probably in his late forties, with salt-and-pepper hair as well as a salt-and-pepper mustache. Though Wade was lean, he also had curves. Wade's man breasts repulsed me as I looked at what could have been described as cleavage.

"What are those papers in your hand?" asked Wade.

"They're just some book I'm working on."

"What's it about?"

"The World Trade Center cover-up. George W. ordered it so he and his boys at Halliburton could make billions of dollars."

Wade raised his eyebrows. "I suppose anything is possible."

"You don't believe me?"

"Obviously I'm no fan of George Bush, but I don't think he commanded airplanes to crash into the World Trade Center."

"Then why did bin Laden do it?"

"I don't think Americans will ever understand that."

I was silent for a minute. It was so difficult to give up a belief that I felt so passionate about only hours earlier. "So you really think that bin Laden is the ring leader?"

"What do I know? I'm in a mental hospital, but then again, so are you. Anyway, I'm going to do my exercises now. I gotta stay healthy."

For the next five minutes I relaxed on the bed as Wade knocked out fifteen push-ups, fifteen sit-ups, and fifteen knee bends. When he was finished, he put his shirt back on.

"I plan on doing twenty of each tomorrow," he said.

"What are you working up to?"

"Depends on how long they keep me here."

"Do you want to leave?"

"Not yet. I'm broke. I already blew my SSI check for September on crack. I come here every few months when I run out of money."

"Don't they care?"

"Who?"

"I don't know. The staff? The nurses? The doctors?"

"Why should they? I keep them in a job. The only people that really care are the social workers."

"Why's that?"

"Since I'm an admitted drug addict, the social workers are obligated to try and get me in a program."

"A program?"

"That's just some bullshit they try to get you to do. Drug rehabilitation or skills training. I always tell them that I'll do it because it buys me some time since they have to do a lot of paperwork and process it. Just before I'm supposed to go, I tell them that I think I've gotten the cure and that I just want to go home."

"They let you do that?"

"They can't make me go to some stupid program," said Wade, shaking his head.

"They could keep you here," I offered.

"That's the thing. I don't care if they keep me here. But they need the bed for someone who's really sick. They always let me out eventually."

"Maybe they won't admit you next time."

"It's a big city with a lot of psych wards. Someone will take me." Wade looked at himself in the mirror and then walked over to his desk and opened a drawer. He pulled out his toothpaste and toothbrush. "Have to keep the few teeth I have left."

3

Shortly before eight o'clock the next morning I was awakened by someone shouting, "Breakfast! Breakfast! Come get your breakfast!" The staff member poked his head in the room. "Come get your breakfast, everyone."

My three roommates and I pushed ourselves out of bed and went one-by-one to the bathroom, then lumbered down the hallway to the common room. By the time I arrived, most people already had their trays and were eating.

The trays were stacked on top of each other in a metal bin that was brought upstairs from the in-house kitchen. On each tray was a piece of paper with the person's name and the type of diet he was on, such as high calorie, low calorie, or diabetic.

"What's your name?" asked the staff member standing by the bin.

I grabbed the tray and looked around the room. I felt like a kid on the first day of school looking for the kids he wanted to hang around with for the next nine months. The difference was, with their unresponsive eyes and imbecilic faces, these people looked more like the kids who rode the short bus to school than the people you would want to have as friends.

Hints of reality like this were helping me recover. Maybe I could ignore people while I was holed up in my apartment writing my book, but in the psych ward, the only privacy I had was when I was in the bathroom. So I was forced to examine my environment and the people inhabiting it. I didn't like what I was seeing. I don't mean to sound like a snob, but most of these people were social outcasts who probably couldn't live on their own without a guardian looking over them.

There were seven rectangular tables with room for four people at each. Unfortunately Wade was sitting at a full table. So I sat down at a table with two strangers. I looked down at my tray. With no preexisting conditions such as diabetes, I was on a "regular" diet, which consisted of apple juice, milk, decaffeinated coffee, cereal, a blueberry muffin, a hard-boiled egg, and a slice of cheese.

I ate everything but the slice of cheese, which looked especially disgusting at this hour of the day. Maybe if the cheese was melted on a sausage biscuit, but a la carte? Apparently other patients felt differently. After finishing my meal, I hadn't taken two steps toward the bin when another patient swooped in and grabbed my cheese just before someone else's hand got to it. Others went through the discarded trays, not caring what they ate.

"Diaz, you can't drink from a milk carton that's already opened," said a staff member.

"But there's still milk left in there."

"That's disgusting, Diaz. Put it back. What if someone spit in his milk?"

"I don't care. I'm hungry."

"You should care. You're not a starving buzzard. Now get away from there and put the milk back."

Diaz looked at the carton of milk like he was saying good-bye to an old friend. He shook his head, probably contemplating whether to obey the order or suck down the rest of the milk and deal with whatever repercussions followed. Reluctantly, he placed the milk back on the tray and slid it back into the bin, then rummaged through the remaining discarded trays for unopened food.

I was heading back to the room feeling lucky one of those sick bastards hadn't tried to gnaw off one of my fingers, when I heard, "Medication! Medication! Come get your medication!"

A long line was already forming in front of the nurses' station. As each person approached, he would hold up his wrist and show his ID bracelet. The nurse would open a drawer where each person's medication was stored for the day. It was painstakingly tedious. These nurses were so slow they would never make it in the fast-food industry, but then again, there was much more at stake in a mental hospital. Dispensing the wrong medication was hardly the same as giving a Filet-O-Fish sandwich to the wrong person.

"You must be new," the nurse said when I got to the front of the line.

"It's my first day," I replied.

"Do you know what medication you will be taking?"

"No idea."

"We're starting you on Celexa and Zyprexa." The nurse handed me a Dixie cup containing one pill. "You'll take the Zyprexa at night."

"No Haldol?"

"We use that to calm people down when they're first admitted. The doctor has now prescribed this. Do you want juice or water?"

"Juice."

I slurped down the pill.

"Raise your tongue, Mr. Humphrey."

"Why?"

"Typically for the first week we make you open your mouth to make sure that you swallowed the pills and aren't just hiding them under your tongue."

At eleven o'clock there was a required meeting for everyone, patients, nurses, doctors, and staff. Thirty people sat in a circle. Caroline, the social worker, led the meeting. She started having everyone, including doctors and patients, introduce themselves.

Then she said, "Thank you for showing up. For those of you who are new, we have an open meeting every Thursday at eleven o'clock. This is an opportunity for everyone to discuss how we can make our living situation a better environment. So, saying that, I will ask the patients what they would like to see changed."

A gray-haired and balding Hispanic man raised his hand. I recognized him as one of the diabetics who scoured the meal trays for extra food. In between meals he shuffled down the hallway from one end to the other muttering to himself with a confused grimace and looking altogether furious with the situation.

"What is it, Mr. Sanchez?" asked Caroline.

Sanchez stood up, looked around the group, waited for everyone to quiet, and then began. "I want more peanut butter and jelly sandwiches for snacks. Every night at snack time we run out of peanut butter and jelly sandwiches, and I have to eat tuna. I don't like tuna. I like peanut butter and jelly."

There were some snickers.

"Okay, Mr. Sanchez. We've been over this before. You only get to eat one peanut butter and jelly sandwich every night. You are diabetic. We can't let you eat as many peanut butter and jelly sandwiches as you want. Your blood sugar will get too high. You don't want that, do you?"

I snorted. What a riot. A sixty-year-old man's biggest concern in life was that he be allowed to eat more peanut butter and jelly sandwiches. He had no questions about when he was leaving or what medication he was taking. No, Sanchez wanted more peanut butter and jelly sandwiches, and his life would be complete.

Across the room, a patient named Muhammad stood up. "Maybe if Sanchez didn't drink all of the milk, we'd save him an extra peanut butter sandwich."

Instead of snickers, this time patients nodded in agreement. Sanchez was not amused. He stomped toward Muhammad with his arms wide and his chin high.

"I like drinking milk with my peanut butter and jelly sandwiches!" he yelled.

"Please sit down, Mr. Sanchez," said Caroline, her voice cracking under the pressure.

"Yes. Please calm down," said Dr. Rider.

Sanchez turned around and walked toward the doctors. "Who are you to tell me to sit down? All I want is more peanut butter and jelly sandwiches! Is that too much to ask?"

"Calm down, Sanchez," Muhammad said. "Like I said, if you wouldn't drink all of the milk, maybe we'd save you an extra peanut butter sandwich."

"You're not telling me how much milk to drink. I decide how much milk I'll drink!"

"You're like a junkyard dog going through the trash. We all like drinking milk with our peanut butter and jelly sandwiches. Fuck you! You'll probably die in here anyway."

"Who are you calling a junkyard dog, you camel jockey?" Sanchez grabbed a chair and slung it above his head, almost losing his balance. His eyes wide and raging, he rushed toward Muhammad like he was going to crush him over the head with the chair. Suddenly another patient flipped a table with a loud thud, and then everyone went scurrying. The women ran to the walls, covered their heads, and shrieked. I looked over at Wade, who was laughing with his snaggletoothed smile. Another table flipped over. One more patient grabbed a chair to protect himself or get in on the action. It was difficult to tell in the chaos.

In the middle of it all, Dr. Rider called out, "Call security!"

Watching from behind a flipped table, I was hoping for a brawl. That would certainly liven things up. The rest of the patients seemed to want one too. They probably just wanted to see two guys mix it up a little bit. Take some of the edge off the place. Blow off some steam.

"You're not going to take that, are you, Sanchez?" a patient called out.

"C'mon, old man! Bring it on! Let's see what you got!" yelled Muhammad with his hands in front of him in a boxer's stance.

Finally, a male staff member flew through the air and rammed Sanchez in the gut with his shoulder. Sanchez tumbled to the floor, the chair crashing down beside him. I looked down at Sanchez, gasping for air and shaking like a stuck pig.

"Calm down, Sanchez," a staff member said as he held him down. Sanchez was making no effort to wrestle free. Everyone circled around to see how badly Sanchez was hurt.

"Give him the needle!" someone called out.

"Yeah, give him the needle," another said.

Sanchez had shaken off the staff member and was now standing. The staff member was hunched over with his hands on his knees, trying to catch his breath but never taking his eyes off Sanchez. Across the room two other staff members were trying to calm down Muhammad, who was excitedly spouting Arabic. Every few seconds Muhammad would lunge in the direction of Sanchez with his arms and legs flying like a windmill.

Three uniformed security guards ran into the unit. When Sanchez saw them, he turned around and calmly walked down the hallway, not daring to look back out of fear he would receive the needle.

"Mr. Sanchez," called out Caroline, "don't come back to this meeting. I want you to stay in your room until you can behave. If you disrupt the meeting, believe me, I will give you the needle."

4

Group therapy sessions were a central part of the curriculum, and there were at least two per day, one in the morning and one in the afternoon. Dr. Rider said, "Attending groups is viewed as being active in one's recovery," but I had a difficult time getting motivated. The meetings seemed so childish.

One day they had bowling as an activity. When I first heard about it, I envisioned private lanes on the top floor of the hospital. I was disappointed when I learned the alley was the hallway, and the ball was hollow and weighed about half a pound. It seemed silly rolling the ball down there and watching the tiny pins tumble with no one even bothering to keep score.

Other activities included art therapy, in which patients would make beaded bracelets or maybe even a collage cutting out photographs and words from the numerous magazines they had on hand. There would be a theme, usually something about expressing our feelings, and at the end of the session everyone would present his work to his peers and explain the meaning of his art. If the work was considered exceptional, the leader would post the art on the walls of the unit. It would have been the same as kindergarten if they had given me a smiley face.

Once a week it would be music therapy, where the group leader brought in instruments like cymbals or a snare drum. They even had an acoustic guitar, which Sanchez showed some aptitude in playing. The leader would pass out words to songs, and everyone sang along.

Though I realized it was in my best interest to participate in these groups, I just couldn't manage it, which didn't necessarily place me in the minority, but it was still frowned upon. The TV was turned off during the groups to further motivate patients to participate.

"Why aren't you in group?" asked Dr. Rider on the third day.

Though I had spoken to the social workers, staff, and nurses, this was the first time since being admitted that I'd spoken with the doctor. "I'm not feeling well," I said.

"Go to group."

"I did. I think that's why I'm sick. I've caught the arrested development that's going around the psych ward."

"It sometimes takes a while for the medication to take effect. I wouldn't get too discouraged. If it doesn't work in the next week or so, we'll switch your medication to something else until we find something that does work."

"Okay."

"Are you hearing voices?"

"No."

"Are you sure? I can't help you unless you're truthful with me. Otherwise we are both wasting our time."

"No. I'm not hearing voices. How many times do I have to tell you?"

"Please try to be patient, Mr. Humphrey. For many people the voices are so commonplace that they don't even realize the voices are disrupting their lives. They accept them as reality and don't realize that we can lessen them or hopefully even eliminate them with medication."

"I'm not hearing voices, but something is the matter with me. My thoughts are scrambled."

"Your asking that question leads me to believe you can live a productive life as long as you stay on your medication."

"Why?"

"Because you have admitted that you have a mental illness. For a lot of people with acute mental disorders, the most difficult aspect is to accept it. Some never come to terms with it."

"What do you mean *acute?*"

"If you are being honest, you have some of the characteristics of bipolar disorder."

"That doesn't sound good."

"Could be worse."

"Like how?"

Dr. Rider raised his eyebrows. "Like some people can't follow a conversation. You seem aware of what is going on around you. Many of the patients can't do that."

"I guess that's good."

"How is your appetite? I heard that you weren't eating. Why is that?"

I was surprised by this comment. I didn't realize my behavior was being documented. "I'm just nervous about everything. I worry that the food is poisoned and someone is trying to kill me, so I just drink the milk and eat the bread."

"So why just the milk and the bread?"

"Because they're sealed, I think they're safe."

"So you admit that you are still paranoid. Are you paranoid about anything else?"

It came like a windfall. "I'm afraid that you're never going to let me leave. I'm scared I'll have to spend the rest of my life locked up in here. I'm afraid you're going to send me to Guantanamo Bay."

"Guantanamo Bay?"

"For exposing the government cover-up."

"I promise that won't happen," said Dr. Rider.

"Really?"

Dr. Rider looked me in the eye. "Beyond a shadow of a doubt."

"That's a relief."

"The real thing I wanted to talk with you about is whether you've made any plans about what you're going to do when you're discharged." Dr. Rider looked at me with welcoming eyes.

"That's the problem. I've got all kinds of things going through my head. I just can't seem to organize them."

"Are you planning on living on the streets?"

"I guess that's my only choice."

"You really have no place to go? No brothers or sisters? No other family members? Because if we could bring your parents on board, your chance of recovery is greatly enhanced."

"I can't."

"Okay, we'll go there later. If you truly have no place to go, we can find shelter for you. We can't discharge you to live on the streets. We have to give you someplace to go. If you want to live on the streets, that's your choice, but we have to give you other options."

"Like SSI?"

"Not necessarily. Are you planning on working when you leave here? You can't have a job if you are on SSI."

"I plan to continue my writing, but right now, it's hard to imagine working a regular job. I couldn't even flip a patty at this point."

"Don't be hard on yourself. You are looking into the future. That is a very good sign."

"What is this SSI everyone talks about and why will I not be eligible if I work?"

"SSI is supplemental security income, and it's for people who are disabled enough that they are incapable of working, and an extreme mental illness can be debilitating enough for someone to qualify."

I thought for a moment. "Well, I'm going to need some money when I get out. I mean, how will I survive without money?"

"I'm really not the one in charge of qualifying patients for SSI. There is much fraud within the program. I don't like to get involved. You need to talk with your social worker."

"But surely you have some input."

"I think it is in your best interest not to worry about it and just concentrate on getting better. Do you still think people are following you?"

"Not recently. But it's easy in here. I don't know how I'll feel when I'm back in the real world."

"In my experience, if you're not paranoid in here, then you probably won't be paranoid on the outside. That is, as long as you take the medication. Do you think the medication is working?"

"Seems to be helping a little."

"Do you still believe that planes didn't crash into the World Trade Center?"

"I don't know."

"Can you explain why the buildings are no longer there?"

I grew quiet. It was such a simple question, but I couldn't answer it. "I know something is strange about those airplanes. I just don't know what."

"I understand. We'll monitor you over the next few weeks and make sure you're stable," said Dr. Rider.

"Next few weeks? How long am I going to be in here?"

"Just relax. We want to make sure you don't end up having to come back here and that you can lead a normal life, which means we need to get your meds right. That takes time."

"I guess I have no choice."

5

By the end of the week there were only two other patients in my room. The fourth patient had been discharged earlier in the day. Despite rooming with him for a week, I never spoke to him. All I knew was that his name was Chandler and that he was an amazing artist. Some of his drawings hung around the unit. He left quietly without saying good-bye to anyone. No one even noticed him leave. That was usually the case. A psych ward is not a place to network. It is a place to endure.

When I woke up, a new patient was in the fourth bed with his head propped up and his eyes wide open. The sheets were pulled up to his chin, revealing a red face and bushy blond hair that looked like it hadn't seen a shower in a good while. When they called for breakfast, I got out of bed and walked down to the dining room. About halfway through the meal, I looked around for the new patient but couldn't find him. I didn't think much of it until I returned to the room and found him still lying on the bed with his eyes wide open and his head propped up.

"Hey, man. Breakfast is here. Go get it."

The patient didn't move. He didn't speak. He didn't even blink. He just lay there looking straight ahead as if he were in a trance. I tried again. "Did you hear me? Your breakfast is ready"

The guy didn't move.

"Okay, suit yourself."

I wasn't about to waste my breath again. I shed down to my boxers and headed to the shower. When I finished showering, James, the staff member who tackled Sanchez, was in the room, standing in front of the new patient's bed.

"Humphrey, have you met your new roommate?"

"Not yet."

"You're not missing much. He doesn't speak. We're calling him Unknown for the time being."

"He didn't eat his breakfast," I said.

"You need to eat your breakfast."

Unknown said nothing.

James looked down at Unknown and said, "We're going to send it back if you don't eat it. You need to eat."

Still nothing.

"All right. Suit yourself, but don't come asking for food later on, because we won't have any."

An hour later after everyone else had taken their morning medication, James came back to the room to speak with Unknown.

"Time to take your medication."

Unknown didn't even make eye contact. He just lay there.

"Mr. Unknown, you need to take your medicine."

Nothing.

All day long, Unknown remained immobile in his bed. He didn't attend a group. He didn't answer questions. He didn't eat. He didn't take his medicine. He hadn't even gone to the bathroom, as far as I knew.

That evening after dinner two staff members, a nurse, and Dr. Rider paid a visit, looking official with their notepads and white coats. Two people stood on each side of Unknown's bed and tried to reason with him.

"You must eat. Do you understand me?" said Dr. Rider.

Nothing.

"We'll talk about the medicine later, but you must eat."

Nothing.

"If you don't take your medicine, we will take you to court so that we can give you injections. Why don't you make things easier on yourself and take the medicine on your own?"

Nothing.

The doctor tried a different angle. "We're going to leave this apple juice by your bed in case you change your mind. Do you hear me?" A staff member held out two cups of juice to make sure Unknown saw them before placing them next to his bed.

"We are very concerned. If you could just see yourself, Mr. Unknown, I know that you would take the medicine. I hate to see you like this. I hate to see you in pain. Don't you understand? We're here to help you."

Still nothing.

"We'll try again tomorrow," Dr. Rider said with a sigh.

The four of them remained standing for a moment longer before filing out of the room.

The next morning Unknown went to breakfast. He didn't sit at a table, but ate by himself in a chair in the corner of the room with his tray in his lap. I looked over at Unknown and saw that he was eating his Cheerios with his hands. There were a lot of people living like animals on the unit, but Mr. Unknown was the king of the jungle.

After breakfast he lay in bed just as he had the previous day. Still refusing to take medicine, he didn't move from that position except at mealtime. By this time people were beginning to notice him.

"He thinks he's God. That's why he's not talking to us. He thinks he's above us," said one of the patients. Everyone at the breakfast table laughed.

On the fourth day James once again came into the room to speak with Unknown. "Since you won't take your medication, we must take you to court. They will decide if you have to take medication. Do you understand? Get up."

Wade, with his vast knowledge of how to beat the system, had already explained the court process to me. He knew this day was coming for Unknown. Once a week the hospital had mental health court for those who refused to take their medicine. It was held on the eighth floor with a judge, bailiff, and everything else related to a normal courtroom. Those who agreed to try their cases in the mental health court signed official letters protesting their incarceration altogether and demanding an immediate release. The judge would bring them in front of the podium, and the residing doctor would present his case, describing the circumstances of the patient's admittance and his behavior since. All of which made the patient look ridiculously ill.

Acting on behalf of the patient, a public defender who probably had barely made it through law school would read some prepared statement, barely making an effort on the part of the patient but going through the motions so the hospital could claim the patient had counsel.

The judge would ask the patient a few questions, such as if he believed himself mentally ill, and of course the patient would deny it. Then the judge would ask the patient something vague, like if he believed anyone was mentally ill. If the patient was especially religious or something, he would reply that only the Lord Jesus Christ could deliver him from evil and that medicine only hindered his mental health. This was all just a formality. Usually the act of defiance kept the patient in the hospital for at least another month until he or she fully understood mental illness is a serious condition that has to be treated with pharmaceuticals.

Unknown wasn't buying any of what James said, and he certainly wasn't getting up. He didn't even speak, but this time he looked at James with raging eyes, but only for a second. Then he seemed to bury his eyes in his skull as he returned to whatever world he was living in.

"I'll bring you some clothes to change into," said James. "Is that all right? If I bring you clothes, will you change into them and go to court?"

An endless supply of donated clothes was available to the patients. Once a week patients were taken down to a room on the fifth floor filled with clothes piled on top of clothes in a mountain of fabric that stood eight feet high. There was no limit to how much a patient could take, and if you were diligent in your search, you might even find brand names, like North Face or Sean John.

Ten minutes later, James returned with a brown bag filled with clothes and set it on the floor beside Unknown's bed. Unknown twisted his head ever so slightly to see what was in the bag before returning his stare to straight ahead.

James looked down and shook his head. "Get dressed. Who knows? If you go to court, maybe they'll let you go home."

"Fat chance of that," said Wade.

James glared at Wade.

But it didn't matter. Unknown wasn't playing this game. He just lay there in bed like he had every day for the past week.

Finally James grew frustrated and left the room without another word, leaving behind the clothes just in case Unknown
changed his mind.

Right after James left, Unknown walked over to the clothes.
He walked over to the clothes, picked up the bag, and shoved it
into the trash can.

That night Dr. Rider, a nurse, and two policemen came into
the room without bothering to knock and proceeded right over
to Unknown's bed.

"Mr. Unknown, are you going to take your medicine?"
Dr. Rider asked with two cups in his hand, one filled with water, the other filled with medicine.

Unknown didn't move and didn't even look up.

"Shake your head yes or no."

Nothing.

"All right. The judge has mandated that we inject you with
Haldol until you take your medicine orally. Roll over."

When Unknown didn't budge, the two policemen reached
down, grabbed his limbs, and forced him to lie on his side.
Unknown didn't struggle, but he didn't surrender either. The
nurse reached over, pulled his pajama pants down, and injected
him in his left butt cheek. Only then did the policemen loosen
their grip.

"It doesn't have to be like this, Mr. Unknown. Hopefully
tomorrow you will take the pills. We don't like doing it this way
any more than you do."

With that comment, they left. It was only Unknown, Wade, and me in the room. Wade, who had not spoken a single word to Unknown for the last week, finally broke his silence.

"I've been coming here for fifteen years, and I'll tell you this much, Mr. Unknown: they will never quit giving you those injections. They will come every night until you take those pills. I hate to be the bearer of bad news, but that's the way it works around here. For better or for worse. So if you want to leave, just take the pills, and when you get out, you can stop. That's what I always do."

"You don't take the medicine when you're not in the hospital?" I asked.

"Hell no! Messes with my sex drive. I can't have that. You know I've gots to have my sex."

"Crack whores?"

"Hell yes, crack whores! Who else is going to hang around me? One time I took a girl I met at the hospital back to my place. After a couple of days I got tired of her and asked her to leave, and you know what the bitch did?"

"What?"

"She tried to burn down my fucking apartment! I don't know about your life, but in mine I have to be careful about the skeezers I bring over. Smoking my crack is bad enough, but I draw the line at burning my shit up. Hell. I'll take a crackhead any day over a mental patient."

I looked over at Unknown and saw a slight smile, the first sign of humanity out of him yet. "Look at Unknown smiling over there. He knows what you're talking about, Wade."

"Hell, everyone does at some level. At least they do in the hood. Unknown, you live in the hood?" asked Wade.

Unknown didn't reply.

"Didn't think so. His high-browed ladies snort the powder and steal the silverware. That's what they do uptown." Wade was kind of chuckling to himself as he looked down at his watch. "Wup, gotta do my exercises."

"How many reps are you up to?" I asked as Wade hopped down to the floor.

"Twenty-five," he said and began pumping.

6

Gilda Smith turned heads when she entered the ward, not only because she looked like a younger Julia Roberts with her auburn hair and large mouth, but because she was making such a commotion with her loud voice. Escorted by two staff members, upon arrival, she broke free from their grasp and ran into the TV room.

"Where's the bartender?" Gilda called out. "This party is too stuffy. I need a drink." Looking around the room with bright, inquisitive eyes, she sat down beside me and rubbed her fingers through my hair. "You're cute. What's your name?"

"No touching, Gilda!" called out a staff member.

Though there was fraternizing between the men and women, touching was not allowed. It was probably the most enforced, along with the most broken, rule on the list. Chronics like Wade were always petting a girl's hand or rubbing his genitals on a woman's rear. Wade called it playing grab-ass with the women. Though he was caught repeatedly, he was never punished. Like Wade said, the staff all knew him, and they also knew he would never take it too far.

"Where's the bartender?" Gilda called out. "I want a drink. In fact, everyone here needs a drink. I'm buying. Order what you want."

All eyes focused on Gilda. I didn't know what to make of her. Apparently no one else did either. What were we supposed to say to a demand like that?

"I say we order a few pitchers of Long Island iced tea. Does that suit everyone?" Gilda looked around the group with her wild blue eyes. "Then it's settled. You! Over there! How about some pitchers of Long Island iced tea?" Gilda looked around the room and began counting aloud the number of people. "Oh, hell. I can't keep up with everyone. How many glasses do we need?"

"There's twenty-seven patients in the unit," I said.

"Then bring twenty-eight glasses. I'm double-fisting it."

Wade raised his eyebrows. It was difficult to tell if Gilda was serious or if she was making light of a serious situation.

"That's enough, Gilda. Come over here and let's get your toiletries," said James.

"You're not the boss. I'm the boss. And I want a pitcher of Long Island iced tea. So bring it now. If they're strong enough, I'll even tip you."

"All right, Gilda. Joke's over. Let's get you settled in."

"Who's joking? I want a drink."

James walked over to Gilda, hooked his arm with hers, and began walking her toward the nurses' station. *Dr. Phil* was on the television but no one was watching. "Come with me. We'll give you a cocktail later. Zyprexa and Lexapro. We call that your cocktail of medication."

Gilda pulled her arm free and ran back over to the TV area. "I'm not taking Zyprexa. I'm allergic to Zyprexa. I'm not taking it. That's all there is to it."

"We'll talk with the doctor about that. He's in charge of your medication. Now let's go."

"Not until you promise me that I don't have to take Zyprexa. It makes me fat and ugly."

"I'm sure if you talk with the doctor, he'll change it."

"That's the way it is around here. Everyone passing you off to someone else. No one taking any responsibility for what happens around here."

James walked over to Gilda and placed his hand on her shoulder.

"Take your fucking hands off me before I throw a suit on you. I'll have my lawyers here so fast you'll be lucky if you're even allowed to scrub the toilets."

James backed five feet way, giving her space. "Gilda, calm down. No one's looking for trouble. You're just a little wound up."

"Quit looking at me like you want to fuck me. I'm not that kind of girl. You hear me? Quit looking at me like that!"

James stood still and waited. Finally, he extended his hand.

"I'm not going anywhere with you, pervert!"

James shook his head. "All right, Gilda. Have it your way. But wouldn't you rather go with me than the police?"

Gilda gave one hard laugh, looked around the room, and started to tear up.

"All right, Gilda. Calm down. Everything is okay," said Maria, a staff member, who had heard the disturbance and come running.

"I don't belong here with these sickos. This is just a big mis-understanding."

"Come here and let me give you your medicine."

"Haven't you heard a word that I've said? I'm not taking medicine. I am allergic to the medicine!"

Maria stared at her.

"Don't tell me you want to fuck me, too! Is everyone here a pervert or lesbian? Tell me that!"

Maria turned her back and walked away. "James, call security. I can't deal with her."

"Fuck you! Fuck you! Fuck you! I'm not taking your medicine!"

I looked over at Wade, who now had an almost indecipherable smile on his face. I was amused and curious as well. I had never seen anyone after they had gotten the needle, or a Thorazine injection, which was much more potent than the Haldol.

Gilda ran to the nurses' station and beat on the counter, screaming, "If you give me the needle, I'll sue you! Think about it! I promise! I'll ruin you!"

Three uniformed security guards dashed through the door.

"She's the one," said Maria, as if there was any question.

Gilda was flailing her arms and stomping her feet. Tears rolled down her blotched face. The guards surrounded her and moved closer inch by inch. Suddenly they grabbed her and dragged her over to the observation room next to the nurses' station.

"Get the fuck off me! Get the fuck away from me! You can't do this to me!" We could hear Gilda's fists beating against the wall as she struggled against the brute strength of the security guards.

Suddenly the security guards filed back out to the main area. One of the guards patted the other on the back and laughed. Apparently Gilda heard the laugh as well. She sprinted out of the observation room, jumped on the laughing security guard's back, and scratched his face with her long fingernails. He leaned forward and shifted his weight to his left so that Gilda rolled off and hit the tile floor.

"Don't you ever laugh at me! You're just a fucking security guard! No one respects you!"

All three guards jumped on top of Gilda and pinned her down. "Get the fuck off me! Get the fuck off me!"

"Take her to back to the room. We're going to strap her down," James yelled.

The three guards lifted Gilda up and carried her back to the observation room. She was screaming and kicking so hard it looked like she was having convulsions.

"Maria, get the straps," called out James.

Gilda was still screaming and pounding on the walls when Maria finally returned with two straps and disappeared into the observation room. More kicking and screaming. Suddenly, quiet. No one made a sound. Everyone stood looking in the direction of where Gilda had disappeared.

A couple of minutes later, the three guards, James, and Maria walked out of the observation room. No one laughed this time. I waited for someone to say something, but no one did. The security guards left the unit. James walked into the TV room, grabbed the remote control, and turned up the volume.

Ironically, Gilda's behavior made me reflect on my own. She was different from the other patients, who were nearly catatonic, barely even strong enough to raise their voices. She was alive and fresh, but obviously disturbed. No one could ever tell me otherwise; nothing she did was rational. Just like when I stripped in the middle of New York City, nothing I did was rational. But still, who wants to believe they are certifiably crazy? No one grows up with that ambition.

7

The next day as dinner approached, most of the patients were either pacing the unit or standing in doorways looking down the long hallway for the first sign of food. As it was a little late this evening, the patients were barely able to control themselves as they watched the second hand on the clock creep toward five thirty.

"Where are they? They're thirty minutes late. They better make up for it with a good meal."

"I hope it's not baked chicken. We always have baked chicken."

"Maybe it will be spaghetti."

"Maybe a cheeseburger."

Finally a black man wearing a light blue shower cap opened the door and wheeled in the bin. The vultures flocked toward the dining area.

"Dinnertime! Dinner!"

Everyone gathered in front of the bin and waited for two staff members to dole out the food, while another staff member went down the hallway to rouse the stragglers. After looking at the paper on each tray, the staff member called out the patient's last name.

"Watson!"

"Brown!"

"Ash!"

When dinner ended, most people congregated in the main room, where the TV was perched high in the corner with chairs lined up in front of it. Always a popular spot whatever the time of day, this was especially true in the evenings, when there were no group meetings or any other distractions. Every night between six and seven, the TV was tuned to the local and national news. That wasn't a preference. It was the rule, and most people watched even if they didn't comprehend it.

Sitting in front of the TV watching ABC anchorwoman Diane Sawyer orate the day's events, with ObamaCare the top news story, I suddenly felt my neck sting like I had just been bitten by an insect. But when I looked down, I saw a rubber band on the floor. I eyeballed everyone to the left, the direction from which the missile had come. Gilda was still hunched in her chair, sleeping, recovering from the Thorazine. The eyes of a middle-aged adolescent I knew only as Baker remained trained on the book he was reading, but he had a smirk on his face. I picked up the rubber band and shot it back, hitting Baker on the knee.

"What did you do that for?" asked Baker, now picking up the rubber band and stretching it between his fingers.

"Just giving it back to you," I replied.

"I don't know what you're talking about." He shot the rubber band back at me.

"How old are you?"

"How old do you think I am?"

"Old enough not to be amused by shooting someone with a rubber band," I said.

"No. Seriously. How old do you think I am?"

Baker was a string bean of human flesh. He had not an ounce of fat on his frame, which gave him a boyish appearance. Obviously, he thought he looked young for his age, but I wasn't going to give him the pleasure of agreeing with him. Judging by Baker's unlined face, he looked about thirty-five, but his bald head, coffee-stained teeth, and sallow skin indicated otherwise.

"Fifty-three," I said.

"What?"

"I don't know. Fifty-one?"

"You really think I look like I'm fifty-one years old?"

"It's just a guess. Why did you ask me if you didn't want to hear what I had to say?"

Baker stood up and turned his narrow body around in a circle with his arms raised. "Be honest. Do I look like I'm fifty-one?"

"Yes."

"Ah hell. You're just messing around. I don't look like I'm even forty-one."

"How old are you?"

"Forty-eight."

"I was close. It must have been your mature demeanor that threw me off."

"Now you're making sense. How old are you?" asked Baker.

"Old enough."

Baker sat down and crossed his skinny legs. I picked up the rubber band and shot it just past his head. He raised the book he was reading to protect his face.

"How long have you been here, Humphrey?"

"Three weeks." I looked at the clock hanging above the TV. It was 6:45. "What book are you reading?" I asked.

Baker looked down at the book. "*The Catcher in the Rye*," he finally said.

"Classic."

"You've read it?"

"Of course.

"Do you read a lot?" asked Baker.

"As much as I can. What's your favorite?"

"*Brothers Karamazov*."

"Damn good read. Do you like Steinbeck?" I asked.

"*Of Mice and Men. Grapes of Wrath. East of Eden.*"

"What about *One Flew Over the Cuckoo's Nest*?"

"First book I read when I decided that I wanted to be literate," said Baker. "Haven't looked back since."

"*The Great Gatsby*?"

"Listen, old sport, I've read everything. Look at these nurses and doctors walking around telling us what to do. They think they're so smart. I'm smarter than them. I wonder how many of them have read *The Brothers Karamazov*."

I could tell by the sly grin on Baker's face that he hadn't had much education. Probably the crowd Baker ran with had never read anything past the sports page, if that. Not that Baker wasn't smart. He was obviously intelligent, just not as intelligent as he thought he was, but I knew the type. Baker was just like my old friend from high school, Shawn Winston. When everyone was filling out college applications, Ol' Winston thought it sounded like a waste of time. He thought he would show us. He wouldn't go to college and he'd still be a millionaire. Winston now worked at Kinko's making copies, and Baker was in a mental hospital reading about Holden Caulfield.

"Reading a lot of books doesn't tell you how smart you are. It just tells you how big of a geek you are," I said.

"Man, I've been here six weeks. I've watched these idiots do their job, and I'm seeing nothing but incompetence. They're nothing but a bunch of pill pushers. I'm stuck in here and haven't spoken to a doctor in over a week. Tell me, what good is this place doing me?"

"Have either of you read Marquis de Sade?" asked Gilda.

"She's alive!" said Baker.

"Barely." Gilda smiled slightly, but in her poor-fitting hospital clothes, and with her wild, unkempt hair, she couldn't disguise her misery.

"Isn't Sade the guy who invented S and M?" I asked.

"Ha. I don't know if he invented it, but the word *sadism* is derived from his name."

"Sounds like light reading," I said.

"Maybe, if you're the devil."

"Is he any good?" asked Baker.

"He's different."

"Bet they don't have his books in the hospital library," I said.

"You might be surprised. *The Catcher in the Rye* was banned when it was first published," said Baker.

"What's Sade's gig? Doesn't he just write about tying up and beating the hell out of some old hags?" I asked.

"It's a little more complex than that," said Gilda. "He wrote about the belief that the greatest sensual pleasure a person can have is by witnessing the misery in others."

"Say what?"

"It kind of makes sense if you think about it," said Gilda.

"I don't think so."

"Be honest. Didn't it give you a little charge when they gave me the shot of Thorazine? Didn't you want to see me when they had me locked up in seclusion and strapped down?"

Her perception shocked me. Not only because it was true, but also because I could scarcely bring myself to admit it. "But it didn't sexually arouse me, I'll tell you that much," I said.

"That's not surprising. You must not be into S and M. Most people into chains and whips have a difficult time being aroused, so they seek comparable stimulation from other activities."

Baker cleared his throat. "I was sexually aroused."

"You probably get aroused when the wind blows," I said.

"Not bad for a forty-eight-year-old man."

I rolled my eyes.

"Do you want to read one of his books?" asked Gilda.

"Marquis de Sade? Sure," I replied.

"My friends are coming by tomorrow. I can get one of them to bring it."

8

Baker wasn't alone in his assessment of the staff, nurses, and doctors. Plenty of other patients thought they were smarter than the doctors, but most of them just talked for the sake of talking. They complained about the food when in reality they had never cooked a hot meal. They talked about their rights, though their rooms were cleaned by both a janitor and cleaning lady once a day. More often than not, they were just repeating things someone else said. It wasn't Club Med, but life wasn't too bad in the psych ward.

The doctors and staff might not comprehend the illnesses as well as they should, but that was not all their fault. Even for a highly trained doctor, it was difficult to understand mental illness without suffering from the ailment. That didn't mean they didn't try. I saw no hidden agendas from any of the staff. There was no "Big Nurse" trying to destroy the patients' psyche. Besides, we weren't entirely cut off from the world. Visitors were welcome twice a day, between one and two in the afternoons and between six thirty and seven thirty in the evenings.

The visiting room was at the far end of the unit, where the Ping-Pong and pool tables were. One of the staff members sat in a chair at the doorway to ensure everything was on the level. Of course, I never received any visitors. When I thought about it, I was saddened. The only way to fight off this depression was to look forward to my freedom.

After dinner Gilda paced the unit as she waited for her visitors. I wanted to speak with her to have some semblance of a normal conversation, maybe talk more about literature or current events. But I did not disturb her. When the staff member announced that Gilda's friends had arrived, she dashed down the hallway to meet them. I snooped around the corner so I could see what they looked like. I was wondering if she had a boyfriend, but with her friends being two girls and one guy, it was difficult to determine.

Now I paced. I didn't know if I was more interested in this strange book Gilda described, which I had always assumed was more pornographic than philosophical, or in talking with Gilda to satisfy both my need and my desire for normal conversation. Finally, I sat in front of the TV and tried to give the questions to *Jeopardy*. After enduring the thirty minutes with the patient sitting next to me doing the same thing but shouting out the wrong questions rather than saying them to himself, Gilda came around the corner with three books in her hand. Without hesitation, she walked over. Now standing next to her for the first time, I realized how tall she was.

"Here it is. The collected works of Marquis de Sade. I recommend you read *The 120 Days of Sodom*. It is his most enduring work."

"I'm looking forward to it. I was intrigued by what you said about us enjoying seeing you get strapped down, but I don't think that is entirely true. I didn't want you to be strapped down."

"But you did want to see it, didn't you?"

"Yes. I did. But maybe I wanted to rescue you."

"Oh yes. You wanted to be my knight in shining armor. Is that it?"

I didn't know what to say. Obviously Gilda was teasing me. "Sounds like you have a fine career ahead of you as a stripper or maybe even a porn star."

"Don't be mean."

"You didn't let me finish."

"Okay."

"You might have a fine career as a stripper or porn star ahead of you except your breasts aren't big enough."

"Ha. You don't think you're a sadist, but you are. Given that you are also homeless, you are a masochist as well. What could be more publicly degrading than being homeless? Why else would you be out there living like that unless you thought you deserved it?"

"I didn't say that I liked being homeless."

"I didn't say that I liked being tied down either."

"I'm sure that Freud would claim that it's because of some childhood experience."

"I don't buy into that bullshit. Just read the book and see what you think. It doesn't have to be for you. Just read it and understand that it's the way some people are."

"Why are you reading Marquis de Sade anyway?"

"Ever since I was diagnosed with bipolar, I've been interested in psychology. I don't only want to know what different people do: I want to know why they do it."

"Funny. I've been thinking about that too the last couple of weeks. That's what makes it so difficult to accept that I have a mental illness. I've never been happier than the three months I was writing my manuscript. It was thrilling believing I was going to be an American hero. I could hardly sleep, I was so excited."

"That's the manic side of the disease. That's how I felt when I first came to the hospital this time. I thought it was a party in my honor."

"Wait a minute. You've been here?"

"This is my third time."

"But how?"

"I don't take my medication."

"Why?" I asked.

"Like I said, I like to feel the way I did when I was admitted."

"You did seem like you were really enjoying yourself at first."

"I want to feel that way all the time," she said.

"But how is that possible?"

"Love, silly."

9

I went back to my room and spent the rest of the evening reading Sade until bedtime at eleven, but even with the lights out I couldn't fall asleep. Maybe it was because I read Sade and was troubled by how cruel the human mind could be. I shouldn't have been reading that material in my weakened state of mind and would have quit reading it sooner if I hadn't wanted to have something to talk about with Gilda.

Around two in the morning, a fourth patient was brought into the room. Through the shadows I could tell only that he was a big guy. He was making a lot of noise by opening and shutting drawers and even had the nerve to turn on the overhead light.

"Hey, dude!" Wade called out.

"I can't see," said the new patient.

"There's nothing to see. Close your eyes and go to sleep."

It was quiet for a minute, and I was just about to fall back asleep when the new guy spoke again. "What time is breakfast?"

"Don't worry big fella. You won't miss it," said Wade.

"Can I get some food now?"

"Hey, dude! Can't you see? We're trying to sleep."

"Sorry."

Wade rolled over and pounded his pillow a couple of times before laying his head back on it. I listened as the new room-mate went to the bathroom with the door open and didn't even bother to flush when he finished.

"Flush the toilet!" I called out.

"I'm sorry. I didn't want to make any noise."

"You've already done that. Now flush the toilet and go to sleep."

"I'm sorry. I really am."

"Go to sleep!"

The next morning I saw a black man, probably in his early twenties with a bowling-ball gut and a faint mustache, stand-ing at the window. He turned around and saw my open eyes. The lights were off, but the rising sun shone through the huge window.

"Hi. I'm Jeff. Sorry I made so much noise last night. I'm just kind of nervous. I've never been in a place like this," he said.

I rose from bed and went to the bathroom. The seat was covered in urine. "Hey, man!" I called out, so furious that I for-got that Wade and Unknown were still sleeping. "Wipe the seat if you're going to piss all over it."

"That wasn't me."

"The hell it wasn't. I'm not touching it. Now get over here and wipe the seat."

Jeff walked over with his big gut peeking below his T-shirt and his pants riding low on his hips. "I'm sorry. I really am. I've just got a lot of things on my mind right now. You know what I'm saying? I've never been in a place like this before."

"We've all got a lot of things on our mind. That's no excuse for pissing on the seat."

Wade rolled over and raised his pillow, propped his head up, and watched the proceedings. Jeff unraveled some toilet paper and wiped the seat. Once again he left the bathroom without flushing.

"Hey! Didn't you forget something?"

"I wiped the seat. Come look."

"Did you flush the toilet?" I asked.

"Oh. I forgot. I'm sorry."

I looked over at Wade, who was still half asleep. Unknown was awake too. It had been five days, and he still wasn't taking his medication, instead having it forcibly administered, but he had begun eating his meals with a knife and fork. In Unknown's case, that was progress.

"Where did you come from?" asked Wade.

"Me?" asked Jeff.

"No, the other guy who came in the middle of the night and woke everyone up," said Wade.

Jeff looked over at Unknown, apparently not catching Wade's joke.

"Oh, for heaven's sake, man. Yes you!" said Wade.

"Oh. I'm sorry. Did I wake you last night?"

"Where did you come from?"

"They brought me up from the emergency room."

Wade sighed. "Before that."

"Oh! I came from the homeless shelter. I got in a fight, and they brought me here."

"What did you get in a fight about?"

"These dudes were making fun of me."

"I can't imagine why," said Wade.

Jeff eyeballed Wade. "I may be slow, but I know when people are picking on me."

"Good for you. It sounds like you're in the right place," said Wade.

"What's that supposed to mean?"

"Nothing. It means just what I said. It sounds like you're in the right place."

Jeff circled the room, keeping his eyes on the floor. Clearly he had something on his mind, and I amused myself by trying to figure out what it could be until breakfast was called. The four of us filed out of the room.

A seat was open beside Gilda, and I took it.

"How far have you gotten in the book?" she asked.

"I'm still reading the introduction. They're describing how the libertines chose their subjects."

"Ha, that's pretty wild, isn't it? They just rounded up virgins to deflower."

"Do you think this really happened?" I asked.

Gilda was eating cereal and didn't speak until she swallowed. "No, I don't think this really happened. It's just one man's fantasy, but I don't think that takes away from the work. It's amazing someone's mind could be so twisted."

"I'll give him that."

"Sade wrote while he was in prison. It wasn't published in his lifetime. He was writing this one hundred years before Freud came up with his views on sex. That's where the genius lies."

"I don't know if I would call it genius. From what I can tell, he belongs in prison."

"Different people like different things."

After morning medication and a shower, I lay down on my bed and began reading more Sade. I couldn't put it down. I kept rereading the parts where the libertines would teach a young girl or boy how to masturbate. I couldn't believe this was not censored. Of course, this was fiction, but it was obscene.

It was giving me a bad vibe, and I was looking for somewhere to release this aggression, so I took a break and went to the bathroom. I looked down into the bowl and couldn't believe my eyes. "Goddamnit! Where's Jeff?" I quickly flushed the toilet and walked back out to the room.

"What's wrong?" Jeff asked. He was looking out the window and biting his fingernails.

"You didn't flush the toilet, *and* you pissed on the seat again."

"How do you know it was me?" Jeff said, walking toward the bathroom.

"Because you're the only one above the age of six who would do that."

Jeff looked down at the toilet. "Looks flushed to me," he said.

"That's because I just flushed it, numbskull. For Chrissakes, dude. You've got to flush the toilet."

"I'm sorry."

"Now wipe off the seat. I need to sit down in there."

"Ah man. Do I have to?"

I stared at Jeff with disbelief. "Hell yes you have to!"

"That's gross."

"You gotta be kidding me if you don't think you're going to clean up that urine."

"All right. All right. Where's the paper towels?"

"Right beside your head. C'mon, dude. Nobody is this dumb."

Jeff stood up straight and looked over at me. "You don't have to be mean about it. I told you. I have a lot of things on my mind. I forgot."

"Listen, I don't care if nuclear warfare is imminent. You've got to flush the toilet."

I watched Jeff wipe the toilet seat and then drop the paper towel in the toilet. "Don't put the paper towels in the toilet. You'll stop it up. Don't you know anything?"

"Where am I supposed to put them?"

"In the trash."

Wade walked in the door, looked around the room, and saw Jeff in the bathroom. "We got this boy potty trained yet?"

"Hey now. I'm a grown man," said Jeff.

"That's what makes it so sad," I said.

Wade took off his blue hospital shirt and laid it on the bed. His man breasts were on display, but obviously he didn't care. He walked to his closet and started straightening out his clothes and toiletries.

"You know that girl giving out the medicine?" asked Jeff.

"You mean Loraine? The big fat one?" said Wade.

"Yeah. I think she likes me," said Jeff.

"That's good. A woman might do you some good. Obviously your mom didn't finish the job," I said.

Jeff walked toward me with his arms wide. "Don't be talking about my mama!"

Wade moved between us and said, "All right, all right. It was just a joke."

Jeff tried to push through Wade. "Tell him to quit picking on me."

Wade turned to me. "Quit picking on him," he said with a smile before facing Jeff once again. "Satisfied?"

Jeff said nothing.

"Now tell us about you and Loraine. Why do you think she likes you?" asked Wade.

"I could just tell by the way she looked at me that she liked what she saw," said Jeff.

"Love at first sight, huh?" said Wade.

"I guess so."

"She's a big one."

"That's the kind of woman I like."

Wade laughed.

"At least those are the ones that like me," said Jeff.

Wade draped his towel over his shoulder and headed toward the shower room. "Jeff, let me ask you something. When was the last time you had sex?"

"Fourteen months ago."

"Fourteen months!" Wade cried out.

"I've been in a homeless shelter. I didn't have a chance. Where could I take them?"

Wade laughed. "But fourteen months. Hell! Get yourself a chicken head. Problem solved."

"I don't want no chicken head."

Suddenly a new voice emerged in the conversation. "What the hell is a chicken head?"

Wade and I both looked at Unknown. In the five days he had been there, Unknown had not said a word. Wade doubled over with laughter. "Finally he speaks because he wants to know what a chicken head is. You're all right, Unknown. You're all right."

"But what is a chicken head?" I asked.

"Crack bitches that will suck your dick for four dollars. Imagine. Same price as a Big Mac," Wade said, as soon as he could catch his breath.

"Why do they call them chicken heads?" I asked, sending Wade into convulsions.

"Because they run from man to man like a chicken with its head cut off," Jeff said.

"That's not the reason. It's because of the way they move their heads when they're sucking your dick."

"I guess it could be that too."

"Why don't you get yourself one?" Wade asked.

"I don't want no chicken head," Jeff said.

"Then don't complain." Wade closed the bathroom door.

"I really gotta get the hell out of this place," Unknown said.

10

Despite the risk for the diabetics, a candy cart came by once a week selling candy bars, gum, hard candy, whatever. Even more than mealtime, the candy cart's arrival was expected, and if for some reason it didn't show at the scheduled time, the patients became agitated. When it did finally arrive, a frenzy shook through the unit as everyone gathered around waving money, their mouths watering, yelling, "Candy cart! Candy cart!"

I had no money, and despite all the food trading that went on at mealtime, no one offered me a deal when it came to candy. The candy intake was a problem for the staff since many patients were diabetic and had to have their blood sugar maintained at a normal level. The next couple of hours boomed with sugar-induced energy as patients danced to music, talked loudly, and smiled a lot. This was followed by a lull when the patients came back down to earth and went to their rooms to sleep it off.

I took this time to change the channel off BET and watch ESPN instead. I had read one hundred pages of the Sade book and still couldn't get over how sick the author was.

"It's hard not to be amused when the libertines' creed was not only that it was proper to do bad things, but even more that they should never do anything good," said Gilda.

"Yeah, but some of these things are sick, like not letting children go to the bathroom so that their behinds get all crusty before they defile them. Call me crazy, but I draw the line at feces."

"Oh, c'mon. That's not your cup of tea? I figured that was right up your alley," said Gilda.

"I like role-playing, but that's just what it is with me. Playing. He's promoting torture. No one would put up with that shit."

"No pun intended," said Gilda and gave me a little nudge.

"Have you read all of this? I don't know if I can finish it. I mean, does he do these awful sexual acts throughout the entire book?"

"It is called *120 Days of Sodom.*"

"Sadism isn't in me," I said.

"Not even a little bit?"

"Well, I'm sure I've got a little bit in me, but it certainly isn't a way of life. Sade believes watching people starve to death would be the ultimate in sexual satisfaction."

"Or putting gunpowder and fuses in people's orifices," said Gilda.

I shook my head. "I haven't gotten to that part yet."

"Keep reading," Gilda said. "I'm not saying it's right, but I want to have a little sadism in me. The rest of the world sure does."

"I don't know if I should run to you or away from you."

"Yes. That's why I want some sadism. Maybe balance me out a little bit."

"I don't think sadism is something we can control. I think that kind of behavior is just a product of a person's makeup."

"Kind of like bipolar," said Gilda.

"Very much."

"But they don't have medicines for sadists."

"I suppose an education is the best way to keep the demons off. Use it to your advantage. Keep busy," I replied.

"For someone so high on education, you certainly didn't go far."

"Where did you go to school?"

"Iowa," Gilda replied.

"Why?"

"I wanted to go somewhere as different from Manhattan as possible. Iowa served a need. Not to mention they have the best writing program in the country."

"Did you graduate?"

"Not even close."

"Me neither."

"Where did you go to school?'

"Boston University."

"What did you study?"

"Nothing."

"You must have studied *something*."

"No, honestly, I didn't study anything."

"But why?"

"I didn't have any idea what I wanted to study in college. I should have taken some years off between high school and college. Gone traveling. Anything would've been better than gambling away twenty thousand dollars on football games. I learned no lesson except that gambling is bad for me."

"You could always go back to school."

"I know. Things are starting to come together in my mind. I can feel myself becoming whole."

"That's great, Humphrey."

"Yeah, it is. Now I want out of here."

"It'll come."

I walked around the unit for a few minutes to stretch my legs. It was the only exercise I could get, unless I wanted to get into Wade's routine of push-ups, sit-ups, and knee bends. So out of shape from being immobile for a month now, I returned to the TV room, where I sat down to read.

A man named Rex sat beside me. He could have sat in any number of chairs that were available around the room, but he was obviously looking for conversation. His hair was rock-'n'-roll long, his body was rock-'n'-roll thin, and his teeth were scarce, maybe from years of abusing speed.

"I just got here," said Rex.

I acted like I was reading the book and didn't hear him.

"I've been in prison for four years."

Good god. What a way to start a conversation.

"That book any good?" asked Rex.

"This sentence I'm reading is great."

"What's it about?"

I looked down at the book, checked the page number, and then closed it. I let out a sigh, not even bothering to camouflage my disdain. "So you just got here, huh?"

"Yeah. Well, last night at least. I spent last night in the ER. I guess everyone has to do that though."

"Must be kind of a letdown to go straight from prison to the nuthouse."

"It's a step up. Came into Penn Station. First thing I got was a whore. Told the ho I'd been locked up for four years and to give me everything I can get for eight dollars."

I was learning a lot about the sordid side of life. "What does eight bucks get you in New York City?"

"Blow job."

"Not bad, I suppose. I heard you can get it for four up in Harlem."

"She wanted ten, but I told her that's all I've got."

"Where did you go?"

"It wasn't easy, but we found a place with steps going to the basement where we had a little bit of privacy."

"Sounds romantic."

"Yeah, right."

"At least she gave you twenty percent off. That was nice of her."

Rex laughed. "Yeah, I got her on special. What about you? You ever go to whores?"

I measured what my response should be before answering. The object was to get out of the conversation with this freak as tactfully as possible. I didn't want to get on Rex's bad side. He looked like he had nothing to lose, and there was no telling what kind of debauchery had seeped into his system while he was locked up.

"I don't go to whores," I answered.

"You should try it. It ain't bad. Once I kept one in Las Vegas for three months straight."

"Three months! How much did that cost you?"

"Three hundred thousand dollars plus all the crack we could smoke."

"You're shitting me."

"No."

"Where the hell did you get all of that money?"

"Dad died and left me his farm upstate. Sold it and went to Vegas."

"You blew your family fortune on prostitutes?"

"And speed," Rex said with that awful smile.

"What are you going to do for money?"

"Got a new plan. I'm going to sue the state of New York."

"For what?"

"Failure to give me medical services while in prison. You see?" Rex brought his hand up to his neck and squeezed it. There was an inflexible bulge sticking out. "I've got a crack pipe wedged in my neck. They were supposed to remove it for me when I was in prison, but they never did, and by law they are required to give me medical services."

"How the hell did you get a crack pipe lodged in your throat?"

"I swallowed it when I saw the cops coming."

"Were you in Vegas?"

"No, this was after that. This was when I came back to New York."

"Is that why you went to jail?"

"No, I got away with the crack. They pinched me later for theft."

"What did you steal?"

"Razor blades."

"You got four years for that?"

"Cops made up some shit that I resisted arrest, and I had priors."

"That's rough."

"They wanted to give me ten years since I was a repeat offender."

"Why didn't they?"

"Lawyer got me a deal. Judge told me that if I copped to being mentally ill, he would cut my sentence in half, so I took it."

"That's all it took?"

"No, that's not all. I had to go to a hospital and have a psych evaluation."

"I imagine that wasn't too difficult of a grift with a crack pipe wedged in your esophagus."

Rex smiled at his luck. "It's kind of painful, but it has come in handy. Will even more so when I get the money from the state."

"Think you'll get it?"

"I don't see how I won't."

This conversation could have probably gone on forever, but I was saved by one beautiful word. "Dinner!"

11

Every Thursday at the mandatory meeting, the staff assigned the patients chores for the upcoming week, like cleaning up the dining room after meals, straightening chairs in the TV room, or calling everyone when meals arrived. Despite the patients' volunteering for each responsibility, and even though there wasn't much else to do, most of the chores went neglected. I ended up wiping the tables down after mealtime and even went one step further by sweeping the floors as well. I didn't do this to gain brownie points from the doctors and staff. I didn't do this because I wanted to show up the other patients. I did this because I felt compelled to keep the unit clean. It had been a long time since I had felt compelled to clean where I lived. My outlook on life in general had improved as well.

Then there was also Jeff's potty training. We weren't making much progress. I had threatened him with diapers if he didn't flush the toilet, and most of the time after he used the bathroom, I had to ask him to wipe the seat. After a week with little improvement, I found a piece of paper and marker made a sign with big red letters that said, FLUSH TOILET AND WIPE THE SEAT AFTER EVERY USE! Pleased with my initiative, I taped the sign just above the toilet and hoped this would remedy our sticky situation.

I lay in bed and waited like a hunter in his deer stand for Jeff to come in and use the bathroom. I played the odds back and forth in my head whether Jeff would abide it. I came to the conclusion that it was fifty-fifty at best. An hour later Jeff walked into the room and went to the bathroom. A minute later Jeff came out without flushing the toilet.

"Damn, Jeff! Can't you read?" I called out.

Jeff stopped with an offended expression on his face. "Of course I can read. What are you talking about?"

"Go back into the bathroom and tell me what it says above the toilet."

Jeff walked back into the bathroom and came back out, but still he did not flush the toilet. I couldn't believe it.

"What does it say?" I asked.

"Who put that up there?" asked Jeff.

"I did."

"Why?"

"So you'd flush the fucking toilet!"

"I flush the toilet."

I let out some air in disbelief. "Go back in there and tell me if the toilet is flushed."

Jeff turned around and went back to the bathroom. The toilet flushed.

"Thank you." I was boiling but let it go. There was no sense in getting bent out of shape with this guy. He was beyond hope. Finally I asked Jeff what he had on his mind that was so pressing he couldn't remember to flush the toilet.

"I need to get some money and get out of here," he said.

"We all want to get out of here, Jeff."

"Yeah, even I'm ready to go," said Wade. "But, Jeff, you have to be patient. You've got to realize they aren't going to let you leave until they're good and ready, so just enjoy yourself. Play grab-ass with the girls. Drink your juice and watch TV. It's not that bad."

"I need to make some money," said Jeff.

"How do you plan on doing that?"

Jeff was now lying on his bed but sat up at the question. "I know this guy who sells winter coats for twenty-five dollars each, and I was thinking if I could get one hundred and fifty dollars together, I would buy six and go back down South and sell them for fifty dollars apiece. I'd double my money. Tell me, Wade, is that a straight hustle or what?"

Jeff looked up with his broad smile like he had a plan that was equal to the invention of the computer. I didn't know if I was more shocked by the stupidity of the plan or the fact that Jeff could do the math and determine his profit margin. However, I realized he had been playing this scenario over and over in his head for the past week and was so proud of himself he couldn't even think straight.

"You're forgetting one thing," said Wade.

"What's that?"

"Where are you from, Jeff?"

"Mississippi."

"How do you plan on getting down to Mississippi?"

"I hear that I can get a free bus ticket over at Port Authority."

"Free bus ticket?" asked Wade.

"That's what they told me over at the shelter."

"That does make your plan possible."

"That's what I think." Jeff lay back down on the bed and put his hands behind his head. He had dollar signs in his eyes. "Wade, how long does it take to get SSI?"

"At least six months."

"Six months! I can't wait that long."

"What do you have to do?"

"In six months it will be spring. Then no one will need these winter coats. I have to get out now."

"I don't know what to tell you, friend. Maybe you'll be able to come up with another hustle in the meantime," said Wade.

"I can't wait that long. I need a Newport. I'm so nervous about this plan working I can barely sleep."

I couldn't hold my tongue any longer. "You mean to tell me that you won't wait it out for your SSI check because you want to smoke a cigarette? I like cigarettes as much as the next man, but hell. I need to think of my future."

"That's exactly what the social worker said to me. She said, 'Mr. Washington, we're going to give you a future.'"

"And they will if you wait it out. It's like hitting the Lottery Pick Three every month for the rest of your life," said Wade.

"But six months?" said Jeff, now pacing the room. His mind was back in motion as he played out all of his good fortune in his head. "I'm going to talk with Caroline right now. Maybe I can get SSI in less than six months."

"You gotta stay on them if you want that check. Those social workers will tell you anything."

Jeff pulled up his baggy pants and walked into the bathroom without closing the door. Instead of using the bathroom, he looked at himself in the mirror for a solid minute, turning his face back and forth so he could see both sides. He took off his ball cap and ran his fingers through his hair for another minute. Finally satisfied, he left the bathroom without turning off the lights.

"Wade, you don't think Caroline will get mad if I ask her about SSI again, do you?"

"Hell no. That's her job."

"Good. I'm going to go talk to her."

"For every person like me that's trying to scam the system," Wade said, as soon as Jeff was out the door, "there's three like Jeff who need a whole team of doctors working on them around the clock, and it still wouldn't do them any good."

"What do you think about his get-rich-quick scam?" I asked.

Wade smiled. "Oh, that? He's just like all of these other boys who come from down South thinking they're going to be able to hustle up some money in the big city. Hell, what he doesn't realize is that he is no kind of hustler, else he wouldn't be in the psych ward in the first place."

12

Plenty of times I thought about what my first meal would be when I was discharged. I was trying to make up my mind between pizza and a cheeseburger. That basic need turned into a motive for finding out how I was going to make money or where I was going to live. I had heard much about SSI, but no one had spoken to me about it. And if Wade was right, it would take six months to get it. Apparently, the system was swamped with paperwork.

Well, there was no way in hell I was going to stay in there for another five months. My mind had cleared up enough to recognize that simple fact, and I felt good that I wanted to get out of the hospital. Many patients seemed to almost enjoy it. Food given to you. Movies to watch. Maybe it was the equivalent of Club Med for some of them.

With the leveling of my mood, I was eager to get back to work. It was amazing how well the medicine worked. I could not deny that in the last five weeks my mind had turned one eighty. I had always been kind of a lazy person in the past, and I

was making progress by maintaining good hygiene despite the
fact that I had a gnarly four-week beard growing. I planned to
let it grow until it came time for discharge. Shaving was a real
pain in the ass from what I could tell. Since razors were involved, a staff member had to be present, and the line took
about thirty minutes. Shaving one month of growth wouldn't
be fun under any circumstances, but with someone watching
sounded miserable. I decided to wait until I was discharged.

One Wednesday morning at the beginning of my fifth week,
I was in the rec room playing Scrabble with two of the other patients when Caroline the social worker approached.

"We need to talk about your discharge. Do you have a minute?" she said.

I looked at the two guys I was playing Scrabble with and
shrugged.

"Should we wait for you?" one of the guys asked.

"It may be a few minutes," said Caroline. Everyone knew a
few minutes could turn into a half hour.

"Go ahead without me. I've got to take care of this," I said.

Caroline led me down the hallway to the dining area. When
we stopped at a table, she signaled for me to sit. She sat down,
placed a huge folder on the table, and opened it. Still not looking at me, Caroline removed papers from the file and placed
them on the table.

"How are you doing?" she asked, her thin lips so horizontal
I could not determine if she was happy, sad, or neutral.

"Best I've felt in a long time."

"Do you think you're ready to be discharged?"

"Where would I go? I don't have anything but the clothes
on my back, and they need to go to the laundry."

"You don't have any money?" asked Caroline.

"You know that. I was homeless before I came here."

"We're not going to put you back on the streets. There are options."

"Like supportive housing?"

"Unfortunately, at this point you are not eligible for supportive housing."

"Why not?"

"You need to be under a doctor's care for six months to determine if your condition is serious enough to warrant SSI and supportive housing."

"Six months?" I slammed my fist on the table. I wanted to get the hell out of the hospital, and no one would give me a straight answer. Wade was always talking about ways he beat the system, and Jeff was trying as well. I really wanted to change my life and get a job and a place to sleep. I just needed someone to give it to me. Someone had to take care of me first before I could begin building that life.

"Calm down, Mr. Humphrey. It's not as bad as it may seem. There are—"

I stood up and pushed my chair back. "I guess that's pretty easy to call from the cheap seats."

"Sit down, Mr. Humphrey. Let's talk about this rationally."

I sat down with my elbows on the table and my hands on my cheeks. "Okay, let's go ahead and talk about this rationally."

"Mr. Humphrey. You need to take a longer-term approach. Rome wasn't built in a day, and neither will your life be. I promise you that we are not going to turn our backs on you."

"So, if had just lain around feeling sorry for myself, I would have a better chance at getting SSI. That doesn't make sense. Shouldn't you be helping the people who have a chance at improving their lives rather than babying those who just want to take advantage of the system?" I realized I needed to shut the hell up, but I couldn't help myself.

"Do you really have no place to go home to?" she asked.

"I'm bipolar. It doesn't get much more serious than that. At one point I believed people were trying to kill me. Just because I cope better than others doesn't mean that I'm doing well."

"Like I said, Mr. Humphrey, we are very proud of you."

"That's great. Maybe you'll drop a quarter in my cup the next time you pass me on the street."

Caroline leaned back in her chair and looked at me with a straight face like she was going to let me vent until I ran out of air. "If you'll listen to me, Mr. Humphrey, you'll realize you have options. We're not going to make you live on the streets. We can place you in a shelter. They have services that can help you get back on your feet. It just takes time, and you'll have to be patient."

"So you're telling me that I can't get SSI?"

"At this point, no, we can't give you SSI, but we can and would like to work with you so that you can get your life back together," said Caroline.

"What does that mean?"

"That's what I came to talk to you about," she said, with a smile creeping across her face again as she pulled out a stack of papers and handed them across the table.

"What's this?"

"A list of homeless shelters in the five boroughs. We can apply for you to live in one of those. You'll have free meals. A caseworker will help you. Job training. Whatever you need to get back on your feet."

"Homeless shelter, huh?"

"Yes. You don't have to sleep on the streets anymore. There will be a place for you. It just takes time."

"How much time?"

"Could be as long as three weeks after we fill out the application."

"So I have to stay here for three more weeks?"

"Not necessarily. There are places known as drop-in centers where you can stay in the meantime."

"What's the difference between a drop-in center and a homeless shelter?"

"A drop-in center is more temporary. You can stay there until we find you a permanent place in a homeless shelter. They will feed you, but the services are limited. The main drawback is that you have to sleep in a chair. They don't have any beds."

"No beds? I'd be better sleeping on the subway."

"It is quiet."

"I want to get out of here, but I want to sleep lying down."

"I understand. You don't have to make a decision right now. Take this list of homeless shelters, and see what you think. I'll come back and talk with you tomorrow or the next day."

13

Still sitting in the dining room, I thumbed through the list of homeless shelters. I noticed that Fort Wellington Men's Shelter was marked with an asterisk and made a mental note to follow up with Caroline about it. I was looking around the room thinking about what I was going to do for the next three weeks when Gilda strolled over to my table.

"You don't look happy. Did Caroline say they were going to start charging you rent?"

I pushed the packet about homeless shelters across the table. When Gilda reached forward, her sleeve rose up, and I saw jagged scars on the inside of her right wrist. Without thinking, I grabbed Gilda's hand and held it still as I examined it closer. She pulled away and covered the scars with her left hand.

"What is that?" I asked.

"Oh, that? Youthful indiscretion."

"Looks a little more serious than that. Did you try to kill yourself?"

Gilda turned to the side so that she was no longer making eye contact.

"You can tell me. I won't judge you," I said gently.

"I have tried to kill myself before, but that's not what it's from."

"Then what is it?"

Gilda turned back around. "I'm a cutter," she said.

"What does that mean?"

"It means I cut myself with a knife."

"Why in the hell would you do that?"

"When I'm in extreme mental pain, I cut myself so that the pain is directed elsewhere, and I only hurt physically rather than emotionally."

"I've never heard of something like that. Does it work?"

"It helps for a little while, but then you have to do it again and again."

I didn't say anything for a minute. That sounded as ludicrous as anything I had heard until I remembered that I was brought in with no clothes. I had improved so much since that moment it felt like another lifetime.

"What's hurting you so bad that you have to cut yourself?" I asked.

"I haven't done it in a while."

"That's good. How long has it been?"

"Almost ten months. That's when I started reading Sade."

Since Gilda gave such an exact number of months, I gathered she was counting the days much like an alcoholic does. "But why?" I asked.

"I'm anorexic as well. I used to cut myself so I would forget I was hungry."

I felt a shiver go up my spine. I had never understood anorexia or bulimia. Then again, I had always been able to eat whatever I wanted and never put on weight. "But you're skinny," I said.

"Thank you."

"Do you think you're fat?"

"That's the thing. The skinnier I got the more weight I wanted to lose."

"But you're eating now, and you're still thin."

"Yeah, but it's always a struggle. That's part of the reason I'm in here. I was having those thoughts again. I took about twenty Paxils so I could fall asleep. That's about the only time I don't feel pain, except of course when I have nightmares."

"Do you have nightmares often?"

"Define often," said Gilda.

"I don't know. Three a week."

"Then I have nightmares often."

I didn't know what to say next.

"I know what you're thinking," said Gilda.

"What's that?"

"That this girl has all kinds of problems."

"Close. I was thinking we all have problems and I need to quit feeling sorry for myself."

"That's good. Maybe I should be a therapist." Gilda laughed. "Instead of the patient telling me their problems, I could tell them mine. Then they would be happy because they have less problems than me."

"What did you do to get sent here?"

"I stalked my ex-boyfriend."

"Ouch. Sorry I asked."

"Yeah, I'm the real deal. The infamous "crazy girl" your friends have warned you about."

"Why did you stalk him?"

"I kept going to his building in the middle of the night to try to catch him with another girl. I buzzed his apartment until he would come down and talk."

"Did you ever catch him?"

"The last time. That's why I'm here. He called the cops."

"Don't worry about it. Just keep going forward. Everyone has those kinds of moments. Life can be hard sometimes."

"I work at Barnes & Noble," said Gilda.

"That's cool. I guess that's why you've read so many books."

"Yeah right. Real cool." Gilda rolled her eyes.

"I'm serious."

Gilda looked me in the eye, probably judging to see if I was being sincere. "That's not all I do. I'm trying to be a writer," she said.

"Don't say that you're trying to be a writer. If you're writing, then you're a writer."

Gilda laughed again.

"What's so funny?"

"Someone else said that exact same thing to me."

"Sounds like a wise person."

"Yes, he was. But I have a reason to say that I'm only trying to be a writer."

"Which is?"

"I never finish the stories I start. I've started something like five books and fifteen short stories and have only finished one, and it was a true story, so that doesn't even really count."

"Of course it counts. Did it get published?"

"I haven't sent it off anywhere."

"Why not?"

"I don't know. I guess I'm nervous that if it gets turned down, I'll get depressed."

"It doesn't sound like you've put everything you have into it."

"It's not easy being a writer with a mental illness. You have to put so much of your soul into your work. It takes a lot out of you. Being that introspective can be a bad thing. Virginia Woolf only wrote one hour a day, standing up the entire time. That's all she could handle, and she still ended up committing suicide."

"Was she schizophrenic?"

"I believe she was probably bipolar."

"Just as bad."

"What's wrong with you?"

"The doctor said I'm bipolar," I said.

"Good. Then we have something in common."

"Maybe we should become blood brothers."

Gilda looked down at her wrist. "Maybe that's not such a good idea."

"Yeah. Sorry. I don't know what I was thinking."

We were silent for a few seconds.

"I'm trying to be a writer too," I finally said.

Gilda's face brightened. "Why didn't you tell me? I didn't know that. What kind of stuff are you writing?"

I hesitated. "It's a book about the government cover-up of the World Trade Center."

"What does that mean?"

"I don't believe airplanes were involved. I think the government made that up for their own agenda."

Gilda bunched her eyebrows. "I was here in New York that day. Trust me. I'm pretty sure it happened."

"It's on the web. Check '9/11 Truth.'"

"Just because it's on the Internet doesn't mean that it's true," said Gilda.

"It was most likely a controlled demolition. Why else would the towers drop as fast as a penny? Steel wouldn't melt like that. Did you see the airplanes hit the buildings?" I asked.

"On TV I did."

"Exactly."

Gilda didn't respond for a minute. "Are you sure this isn't a symptom of bipolar? I don't want to doubt your premise, but as your friend, I can tell you that will be a tough sell."

I looked down and shook my head. "I know. I know. I've been thinking the same thing the past couple of weeks, but it is so ingrained in my mind. I mean, I've written about three hundred pages on the subject. I can't just dismiss it."

"I understand, but don't feel bad. I'm sure you're not completely wrong. I'm sure the government isn't being totally honest with us. I'm sure there is a story there. It just might not be that big of a story. That would be a pretty big hoax to pull on the whole world." Gilda laughed.

"But I'm not the only one who believes that. There are a whole lot of celebrities like Charlie Sheen and Jesse Ventura who believe it, too."

"Why am I not surprised that a professional wrestler would think it was a hoax? Besides, there are plenty of people who don't believe man has ever landed on the moon, but I do."

"You've got to understand one thing. When I was writing my book on the cover-up, it was the happiest time of my life. I was writing fifteen hours a day, sometimes more. I thought I was going to change the world. I honestly thought I was going to be the president of the United States. I've never even considered that idea before that. Then suddenly I was president. I didn't even have a choice in the matter."

"You don't seem like a homeless person."

"Why do you say that?"

"You are far too normal."

"Like how?" I asked.

"For one, you shower twice a day."

"You go without showering for a week, and see how often you do it when you get the chance."

"But how did it happen?"

"Lost my job. Lost my apartment. Estranged from my family. I had nowhere to go."

"What happened between you and your parents?" Gilda asked.

"I stole my college tuition money from them."

"And they don't want to see you again?'

"It goes both ways. I don't want to go back until I can at least pay back some of the money. I can't just show up at their door with mental health issues and start living there."

"How long has it been since you've seen them?"

"Two years."

"What would you say if you saw them?"

"That I'm sorry."

"Then do it," said Gilda.

"I'm ashamed."

"Like I said, you're masochistic too," she said.

"Is that why you enjoy reading Sade?"

"I'm trying to understand why people treat me the way they do." She looked away. I looked in the same direction and saw one of the patients curled up in the fetal position on the cold, hard floor. Things like this were so commonplace that it wasn't even worthy of comment.

"What are you planning on doing when you get out?" asked Gilda.

"Get a job and try to put my life back together."

"What kind of job?"

"I don't know."

"Where have you worked?"

"I worked at Foot Locker for a while, but I got fired."

"For what?"

"I started giving the shoes away. That was four months ago."

"That's all right. You were sick."

"It was still stupid."

"But retail? Maybe I could get you a job at Barnes & Noble. That is, if they take me back."

My heart leaped. "You would do that for me?"

"Why not? I'm sure you can handle it. It's not exactly what I call difficult. Can you work a cash register?"

"Yeah."

"Can you recommend books?"

"Yeah."

"Can you count to a hundred?"

I looked at her funny.

"Have to be able to count the change." She smiled.

"I guess that's true."

"So you're in?" asked Gilda.

"When I get out, I'm in."

14

Though Unknown had begun taking his medication, he was still somewhat withdrawn. Sometimes he was outgoing and engaging, other times he wouldn't even answer basic questions such as whether he wanted the next shower. This was especially true at mealtime when other patients wanted his food. For some reason he would not trade food. In fact, he wouldn't even acknowledge people when they asked, instead glaring at the inquisitor with his dark, sunken eyes.

The more resourceful scavengers watched Unknown eat throughout the meal, never taking their eyes off him until he stood up to walk his tray over to the garbage bin. Then several patients jumped at once and grabbed his leftovers, the quickest hands winning the prize.

"Beggars!" Unknown would yell.

But it made no difference. The next mealtime, the waiting game began again.

The only other time Unknown responded was at medication time.

"Here's your medication, Unknown. Do you want juice or water?"

"Water."

After breakfast came shower time. In spite of there being twenty-seven patients on the ward, there was never a line for a shower. Each room had its own shower, so crowding wasn't a valid excuse. The showers were hot and had good water pressure, but still only about half the patients showered on a regular basis. The staff constantly battled to get the surliest of patients to bathe, and there was no shortage of greasy stringy hair, and the smell of a funk was what you'd expect in a gym locker room. I couldn't understand it. Showering was practically the only pleasure a man could find on the ward.

The staff knew of the problem, so the one television on the ward wasn't turned on until ten o'clock every morning. It's safe to say everyone would have enjoyed watching Jerry Springer, but it was forbidden because the patients got too excited, which led to fights. In fact, a list of rules was posted in the common room. One of those rules was "Absolutely No Jerry Springer."

Now that Gilda had given me a job prospect, I was giddy to get out of there and away from these freaks. The scavengers were annoying but so pitiful it was barely worth the energy thinking about them. The ones that really irked me were the "God Squad," the patients who believe they were either God or the second coming of Jesus Christ.

Despite their grandiose beliefs, they weren't easy to pick out from the other patients. They talked to themselves and paced like many of the others, but they weren't running around the unit trying to save everyone. It was more like their little secret, like they didn't want anyone else to know. Only if you asked them questions did you realize what was on their minds.

It wasn't in my nature to buddy up to them, but Gilda felt sorry for them and was always trying to help.

One patient, a twenty-one-year-old man, thought he would be known as Jesus Christ when he turned thirty-three years old. He cried as he told Gilda how his girlfriend committed suicide to prove her love for him since he wouldn't have sex with her because he had to remain pure to fulfill his destiny. Somehow he thought that he was a modern savior, and due to the changing times, his disciples would be women.

Gilda enjoyed playing her role as the resident Mother Teresa. She drew pictures for the troubled young man and once wrote him a letter telling him it was all right to grieve for his lost love. I wasn't buying any of it.

"Don't you know that the only people who lie more than the mentally ill are gamblers and prostitutes?" I asked her.

"But he thinks he is telling the truth," Gilda replied.

"Do you think it helps to go along with his theory? You are just strengthening his conviction, making it more difficult for him to come to terms with reality."

"I'm only trying to be there for him. I haven't told him that I believe he is Jesus Christ. I'm trying to show him that he is human and it's all right not to be perfect."

"That should be apparent enough. After all, he's in a mental hospital."

"You are too."

"Yes, but I don't think I'm a deity."

"But you don't believe that airplanes crashed into the World Trade Center either."

"No, you're wrong. I used to think that. I don't anymore. Besides, everyone told me I was mistaken and that I was wasting my time. Why can't you do that with him?"

"So you admit that you were wrong, that it really was air-planes?"

I sat very still for a moment before finally saying, "Yes."

"That's great. It really is. I can only imagine how hard it was to relinquish that idea, but I think it's a very big step for you."

"But don't you see? That guy's in the same position I was in, and you're making it worse for him by satisfying some kind of need to nurture."

"Sometimes you can be very cold."

"And sometimes you can be very naïve."

"Just because I'm nice doesn't mean I'm naïve," said Gilda, crossing her arms.

"But don't you understand? You're not helping him. You're hurting him."

"Listening to someone talk about their problems can never be hurting someone."

"That's not your job. You're a patient."

"Obviously you will never be a doctor. You don't want to help people."

"That's not true. I want to help people that can be helped. Some of these people aren't even making an effort to be pro-ductive."

"Like your friend Wade?"

"Wade is looking out for Wade."

"But he's okay?"

"Listen, Wade and I will never speak again once he leaves this hospital. He knows that. I know that. That is, if either of us even cares. We're just passing time."

With that, Gilda got up and walked away. I couldn't make up my mind if I was frustrated by the lack of attention Gilda was giving me or if I was maddened by the fact she seemed to be buying this guy's bullshit. Whichever. I wasn't disguising my unhappiness very well.

"You know that girl loves you," said Wade.

"Who?"

"Gilda."

"Why do you say that?"

"I can just tell."

"Really?"

"Don't you understand? She's an angel. Let her do what she thinks is right. She's not doing it for herself. She's doing it because she believes she's helping him."

"Do you think she is helping him?"

"A beautiful, intelligent woman showering him with attention can't be a bad thing. He's just sick. Not everyone here is pulling a scam. Most of these people have real problems."

"I know, I know. This place is just getting to me. I need to get out of here."

"Yeah. I'm leaving tomorrow," said Wade.

"Congratulations. You gonna get yourself a chicken head to celebrate?"

"Most likely."

I found Gilda sitting at a table by herself flipping through a magazine. Her hair was pulled back in a ponytail, and for the first time I had an unobstructed view of her long neck. *Am I in love with Gilda, or am I just lonely?*

Gilda looked up at me with her deep blue eyes and asked, "Are you mad at me?"

I was caught off guard. "Why would I be mad at you?"

"I don't know. Because I spend my time feeling sorry for these people."

"That's no reason to apologize. I should be apologizing to you. I'm the one in the wrong here."

"You really think so?"

"Definitely. It's just not in my nature to help someone I don't know. I should really work on that."

"It has its drawbacks," Gilda said.

"Like how?"

"It's not healthy to get emotionally involved with people you barely even know."

"Why?"

"It makes you appear less genuine about caring for the problems of the people you do care about."

"I don't know about that. Maybe I've just become numb to the pain of others."

Gilda's eyes and lips looked soft and sensual. "You have a lot of pain in your life right now. You probably don't have the emotional energy to help someone else out. Everything you have is in your own fight for survival." She meant what she said, and I felt a twinge of guilt.

"You shouldn't waste your time on something as self-absorbed as writing. You should be a nurse or a psychiatrist," I said.

"I like to think I'm helping people with my writing. I'm trying to reach people who feel similar to me."

"That seems kind of naïve." I leaned forward and shook my head in disbelief. "I'm sorry. I shouldn't have said that. That's noble. I wish I had a calling like that."

"Maybe you will, and you just don't know it yet."

"Still. I shouldn't have said it."

"That's all right. If that's what you believe, then you shouldn't apologize."

"I don't know if that's what I believe. Sometimes I speak without even thinking about who I might hurt."

"Usually the first instinct is the right one."

"I don't know about that. Sometimes I think I should do the exact opposite of what I feel is right."

Gilda laughed a little and laid the magazine down on the table.

"What's so funny?" I asked.

"I don't know. Doing the exact opposite of what you feel seems like a funny way to go through life."

"I am homeless. Obviously I haven't used my best judgment."

"You're overdoing it. You were homeless for three days. You just don't have the backups like everyone else. Do you mind my asking where your parents live?"

"Springfield."

"Massachusetts?"

"Yeah."

"Do you have any brothers or sisters?"

"I'm an only child."

"Good god. You're an only child and you ran away."

"More like Ol' Arnold shoved me out. He and my mom didn't want to have anything more to do with me either."

"Your dad's name is Arnold, too?"

"Yeah, I'm the third."

"When was the last time you called them?"

"I'm not calling them and telling them that I'm in a mental hospital, I'll tell you that much. Maybe when I get on my feet, but not now."

"But they could help."

"They've already tried to help me once by paying for my college, and then I stole from them."

"Did you bankrupt them?"

"No."

"What does your dad do?"

"Real estate appraiser."

"Does he make a lot of money?"

"Not enough for me to steal from them for a year and a half."

"Why did you do it?"

"I don't know. Actually I do know. My first semester the guy across the hall gave me the number of a bookie, and I lost a lot of money when I went zero for eleven on the college bowl games. I didn't have the money so I used the tuition money to pay it off and then kept the rest for me to live on, which led to more gambling. I always planned to pay them back when I had that huge weekend and won ten thousand dollars. And then it went to twenty thousand, and I realized I wasn't going to pay them back anytime soon."

"How did they find out?"

"They finally asked to see my report card."

"That would do it."

15

When I opened my eyes the next morning, Wade was changing out of his pajamas and into his street clothes.

"I'm out of here," he said.

"You think you'll check yourself back in before I leave?"

"That would be a no. I've got two months' worth of SSI checks waiting on me. That'll pay for a lot of chicken heads."

Wade shoved his remaining clothes into a garbage bag and, without shaking hands or even saying good-bye, walked out of the room. Now that Wade had been discharged, I was ready to embark on my new life. I had done enough collages, bowled enough strikes, and made enough beaded bracelets to last a lifetime. It was Friday afternoon, and I knew if I didn't speak with Caroline before the end of the day, I would have to wait until Monday to discuss it further.

When I looked across the room, Sanchez was lying down on a bed with a *People* magazine open and his right hand stuffed down his pants.

"That's disgusting, Sanchez."

"Don't watch."

I averted my eyes and walked back down to the TV room. Gilda sat in a chair with her legs pulled up to her body. Her hair was covered by a purple bandana that matched her purple slippers. I couldn't put my finger on it, but she seemed to have a glow about her. I sat down next to her.

"They're discharging me on Monday," said Gilda.

"That explains it."

Gilda placed her hand on my head and stroked my hair. "What's wrong? Aren't you happy for me?"

"Of course I am. It's just that all my friends are leaving me, and I'm stuck in here having to deal with these loons by myself."

"Don't worry. I'll come back to visit you."

"And you won't forget about the job at Barnes & Noble, will you? I'm counting on it."

"I'll do what I can."

That afternoon around four I met with Caroline and Dr. Rider in the doctor's office. I wasn't nervous anymore. I knew where I was going. I just had to wait it out.

"How are you doing, Mr. Humphrey?" asked Dr. Rider.

"Some days are better than others."

"Do you think the medicine is working?"

"Yes."

He reached on his desk and opened a manila folder. He flipped through the pages until he found what he was looking for. "You're taking Zyprexa and Celexa. Is that right?"

"I believe so."

"I understand Caroline has discussed your discharge. What are your plans?"

"Going to a homeless shelter."

"You do realize it could be as long as three weeks before you're discharged. There is a lot of paperwork and processing to go through in order to secure you a bunk in a homeless shelter. Is that okay with you?"

"I was hoping you would tell me."

"Are you planning on taking your medicine when you are discharged?" asked Dr. Rider.

"Of course."

Caroline interrupted. "I guess what we're asking is how were you planning on paying for your medication?"

"I don't know. I don't have any money."

"That's why we're asking."

"How much does it cost?"

"We can get each prescription for you for as little as three dollars a month—basically a token payment. But that's as low as we can go. Since you're taking two medications, it'll be six dollars every month," she said.

"I don't know how I can do that."

"Are you planning on working?"

"I hope to, but I don't know how long it will take me to find a job."

"We can give you a month of prescriptions when you leave, but you'll need to pay after that."

"I guess I could panhandle or hustle up some money."

"So you're okay with that?" asked Dr. Rider.

"I guess I have to be."

"What about your book? How do you feel about it now that you have been in here for a month?"

"Well," I said with a smile, "I'm not sure what I believe, but I think it's safe to say some things had been a little misconstrued in my mind."

"You know you can't drink alcohol or use street drugs when you're taking this medication."

"I don't think that will be a problem."

"Why do you say that?" asked Dr. Rider.

"I don't have any money to pay for them." I let out a light laugh.

Dr. Rider smiled. "People have a way of finding the money if they want it badly enough."

"Just the same. I'm not planning on it. Drinking or using drugs is not going to help my situation any."

"And what is your situation?"

"I'm bipolar."

"Do you believe that?"

"That's what you told me."

"But do you believe it?"

"I know something is wrong with me."

"That's far different from how you felt when you were admitted."

I thought about my state of mind in those days. And though I had just been diagnosed with bipolar, I had suffered for a long time. Even back when I stole the money from my parents. That's something I wouldn't have considered two years before or now. I appreciated what the doctors had done.

"And thanks," I said, offering my hand to shake. "You've changed my life. Actually, you have given me a chance at life. I think I can make it."

"Just stay on your medication. Ninety-five percent of the patients who come back have quit taking their medication. You're a smart person. Don't make that mistake."

I returned to my room and grabbed my manuscript out of the closet. I flipped through it, looking at some of the more outrageous claims. I had devoted three months of my life to this project. I had lost my apartment because of my total belief. Now I had finally concluded that the entire premise of the book was 100 percent wrong. Seeing no reason to keep it and wanting to move forward with my life, I dropped the manuscript into the trash can. I thought the symbolic act would make me feel better, but it didn't. I still couldn't get over how much time I had wasted on something so ridiculous.

16

When Gilda left three days later, I watched her walk across First Avenue from my window on the tenth floor. Though she looked the size of an ant, I could see her turn and wave before continuing down the street. As I walked back over to my bed to lie down, I thought the chances were about fifty-fifty that I would see Gilda again. Friendships made in a mental hospital were better characterized as convenient rather than lasting. Most people preferred to remain solitary, with the exception of the younger patients, who were just green enough to treat the odyssey more like a summer camp than a sanitarium.

Two patients annoyed me to the point of disgust. I labeled them Tweedledee and Tweedledum, though their real names were Mike and Noah. Mike was an eighteen- or nineteen-year-old black kid with a faint moustache, blue jeans riding low, and a blabbering mouth. Noah, who took Wade's bunk, was a sixteen-year-old Hispanic kid with big flapping lips that were always open, as he breathed through his mouth, giving him an imbecilic look. They were admitted at about the same time and had fused together in my mind.

"I have a gift with the ladies," said Mike.

"I do too," said Noah, who was sitting next to Mike in the TV room.

"Women just love me. They can't help themselves, and I can't say no to them. I love them so much."

"I do too," said Noah. "The girls say that I'm a male slut. They say I'll fuck anything."

"That's what they say about me too."

Noah held up his fist and waited for Mike to bump it. "Ahh, snap."

"Let me show you how it's done," said Noah.

"Go ahead, brother. Enlighten me."

Noah walked across the room and sat next to a young woman who was so quiet that I had assumed she was mildly retarded. "Do you want to braid my hair?" asked Noah.

The girl giggled, too embarrassed to even make eye contact.

"Well, do you?" Noah looked at Mike with a sheepish grin on his face.

The girl giggled again, but it was clear she wasn't going to braid Noah's hair. But he was not deterred. "That's why I've got long hair. It drives the women wild. Always a good line to introduce myself to the ladies. Never fails."

I couldn't take it any longer.

"Looks like you're zero for one in my book."

Mike and Noah looked at each other and died laughing. "We got ourselves a hater. Don't worry, pops. You're not any different than the others. Just like all the women love me, all the men hate me." Mike laughed to the point it became obvious he was forcing himself rather than being honestly amused.

I wouldn't give up.

"You two look pretty good together. Are you sure you aren't—"

"Don't even say it, bro. Don't even say it."

I returned to my room. Soon enough Mike and Noah were in the bathroom smoking cigarettes, which was the only time these jokers shut the hell up, so I didn't complain, but smoke seeped out the crack under the door and into the hallway. Just after they left the bathroom, Trudy, a staff member, walked into the room. She sniffed around the bathroom like there was any question about what was going on.

"Who's smoking?" she asked.

Both Noah and Mike looked down at their feet and mumbled.

"Humphrey! Are you smoking?"

"Not me."

"Then who is?"

I waited a second. "I don't know."

"Someone's smoking in here, and I aim to find out. I'm calling up security. We're going to search the room. Don't go anywhere. Any of you. You hear?"

When Trudy left, Mike and Noah cracked up at the thought of being searched for cigarettes, which even I had to admit was mildly amusing. At least it was something out of the ordinary to pass the time. I didn't believe a search was really going to happen, but Mike and Noah weren't taking any chances.

"Flush the matches down the toilet," said Mike.

"Then we won't have any fire," said Noah.

"You hold the matches and we won't have fire either."

"True that."

Noah walked back into the bathroom and flushed the toilet. A moment later he came out.

"Did they go down?" asked Mike.

"Yeah, they went down."

Just as I was sure Trudy's statement had been made in vain, two security guards walked into the room.

"Everyone, stand by your bed."

"This isn't my room," said Mike.

"Then go to your room," said the security guard. "We're searching the entire ward. It's against the law to smoke in a hospital."

I stood by my bed. One security guard inspected my side of the room while the other searched Unknown and Noah's side. They looked in the closet and shook the folded clothes in their search for the contraband then threw them back into the closet with no remorse. They stripped the sheets and looked under the mattresses. They pulled out the desk drawers and felt all around.

"Now we're going to search you," said one security guard, "because we can smell the smoke. Someone was smoking in this bathroom and we're going to find out who it was."

I felt the guard's breath brush up against my nose as he said, "Put your hands against the wall."

I abided.

"Spread your legs."

Once again I abided.

"How long you been in here?" asked the guard as he frisked me.

"Since September fifth."

"Were you smoking?"

"No."

"Do you know who was smoking?"

"No."

The guard patted me on the back. "He's clean. What about that one?"

"Same."

"Let's go on to the next room."

Afterward Noah bent over laughing. "You're all right, Humphrey. I thought you were going to rat us out for sure."

"No big deal."

"No big deal? I don't know about that. Wait, let me give you something." Noah walked over to his closet and pulled out a bag of candy. "Here you go. Have yourself a lollipop on me. You got us out of a jam."

I never knew where Noah and Mike hid the tobacco, but after lights out at eleven o'clock, they were back in the bathroom smoking again. With the two laughing and carrying on so much, I wondered if they were smoking pot rather than tobacco. Though I wasn't that much older, I wondered where they got the energy to carry on like that.

I guessed it didn't matter. I was a teenager once too. Only I didn't remember high school being such a happy time.

17

Three days after Gilda's discharge I had a visitor. Having no doubt who it was, I hurried down the hallway to the visiting room. Wearing aqua pants and a pink-and-white striped blouse with her auburn hair down and a touch of pink lipstick, Gilda greeted me with a pearly smile, but even more fetching was the bag of Taco Bell in her hand. When she saw me, she extended her arms, offering a hug. Human contact was a rare treat, since touching was prohibited between patients.

"Taco Bell!"

"I thought you would like that," Gilda said as she handed over the bag.

"Mr. Humphrey, you need to sign in," the attending staff member said as we started to sit down.

"Of course." I signed my name and returned to Gilda, who was sitting at a table with a fire in her eyes I had never seen before.

"You look good. How does freedom feel?"

"Kinda strange. It took a couple of days to get my groove back. That's why I haven't visited you yet. I hope you're not mad."

I laughed. "Gilda, I wouldn't have blamed you if you never came back. Frankly, I want to forget this place ever existed." The light in Gilda's eyes switched off, and the corners of her mouth turned down.

"What's wrong?"

"I don't know. I guess I don't have such bad memories. It was the right place for me at the right time."

"Well, in any case it's certainly not Shangri-la," I replied, and my mind drifted to when Wade had said the same thing on the first day I was admitted.

"Which reminds me, I brought a book for you. I thought you might like *Venus in Furs*."

"Never heard of it."

"The author's name is Masoch. It's where *masochism* is from," she said.

"Good?"

"Kind of depressing really, but I thought you might enjoy reading the flip side to Sade."

"Why would I want to read something depressing when I'm in the mental hospital?"

"I don't know. I see some masochistic qualities in you that I thought you might like to be made aware of."

"Like how?"

"Like punishing yourself by staying away from your parents. I don't think you like the pain, and I don't think your parents like inflicting it. Get a fresh start."

I unwrapped a gordita and took a bite, tasting the salty meat that had been missing from my diet. "Did you get your job back at Barnes & Noble?" I asked, chewing my food.

"Okay, okay. You don't want to talk about your parents. But you need to call. If not for you, for them. Just consider it."

"Maybe I will."

"Good. That's what I wanted to hear. You're stubborn, but you come around. I've seen worse."

"I don't hate them. I'm just ashamed. I stole a lot of money."

"Oh! I haven't forgotten about the job, Humphrey, but I'm going to wait until you're discharged."

"Did you tell him where you've been?"

"Ha! Not even I'm that honest. I told my boss I had walking pneumonia."

"And he bought it?"

"What's he going to do, call me a liar? In any case, it sure as hell beat telling him the truth. He's pretty cool, but I don't know how he would respond to this place."

"Yeah, I suppose so."

The conversation stopped as I unwrapped the second course, a beef Meximelt. I looked around at the other two patients with visitors. There was a young Hispanic woman visiting her mother at one table. On the other side was a male patient, obviously gay. I knew this because he wanted to be called Marilyn Monroe, which he requested with a lisp. He weighed at least 250 pounds and had a raspy goatee and frizzy hair. The staff called him Mr. Harvey, his last name.

"When do you think you're getting out of here?" asked Gilda.

"Sometime in the next three weeks, they tell me, but it could happen at any moment. Supposedly, I only have three hours from the time they tell me to get to the homeless shelter."

"Three hours? That seems kind of ridiculous, don't you think?"

"Actually it seems about par for the course."

Suddenly, Marilyn Monroe stood up and started yelling at his visitor. "You have no right to say that to me. I'm a grown woman. You can't tell me how to live my life. That is the only thing truly mine in this world."

The elderly woman sat motionless. She didn't even blink as Marilyn threw his tantrum, and she moved only her head when Marilyn heaved his fountain drink at her. The cup exploded on the floor next to my feet.

The on-duty staff member raced into the room. "Calm down, Mr. Harvey!" she called out, but Marilyn didn't listen. He towered over the old woman, yelling, "Get out of here! Leave me alone!"

"Mr. Harvey, this is not acceptable," said the staff member.

"Tell her to leave! I don't want her here!"

The staff member looked at Marilyn's visitor.

"You really want me to leave?" the woman asked Marilyn.

"I said it, didn't I?"

Without saying a word, the woman picked up her purse, pushed her chair under the table, and walked out of the room.

"Mr. Harvey, it's time for you to return to the other patients," said the staff member.

His head held high, Marilyn marched out of the visitor room.

I looked at Gilda. "Like I said. Nothing really surprises me in this place. When I get out of here, it will probably take me a while to get used to the boredom of normal life."

"That's what I was trying to tell you. It is difficult to adjust. I kind of understand how criminals locked up for twenty years have a difficult time immersing themselves back into the general population," said Gilda.

"I don't think that will be a problem for me. I'm not planning on coming back here."

"I don't think anyone plans on coming back here. It just kind of happens."

"Do you think you'll be back?" I asked.

"No. I don't. I've learned a lot about myself by hearing your story, and I realize that some people have to take medication to function in society. I am one of those people. That's a fact. I will take medication for the rest of my life. And if I can save you some heartache, I'm telling you: take your medication every day for the rest of your life, or you'll end up right back here."

"I know. I need a job just to pay for my meds. They cost me six dollars a month."

"That seems fair."

"Do you really think you'll be able to get me a job?" I asked.

"I don't know if I can get you one, but I can put in a good word for you. With the economy and the job market the way it is, everyone and his brother are applying for jobs. People who were making a hundred thousand a year before the recession are now applying for nine-dollar-an-hour jobs at bookstores."

"I guess I'm a little underqualified compared to them."

"More like they're overqualified. An MBA doesn't help you be a better cashier. Management doesn't want to hire someone who is going to leave quickly. They want to lock someone into the job for years rather than a couple of months."

"Is that what I'll be? A cashier?"

"What did you think, you were going into management?" asked Gilda.

"I guess there's not a lot of layers at the operational level."

"That's all right, isn't it?"

"Sure. Beggars can't be choosers."

"Speaking of which, what are you going to wear? How are you planning on using the subway? What are you going to do

for money before you have a job? You don't have any, do you?"
asked Gilda.

"Caroline told me I'll get a one-way subway ticket to go to
the shelter."

"But how are you planning on going anywhere else? You're
not planning on hoofing it everywhere, are you?"

"I hope not. I've been so inactive the last six weeks; I probably can't even walk up a flight of stairs."

"Then what are you planning on doing? You can't get by on
no money."

"I guess I'll panhandle."

Gilda shook her head. "I can't let you do that. I'll loan you
money."

"But how will I pay you back?"

"When you get your first paycheck, silly."

I smiled at her. "That's awful nice of you. Twenty dollars
would go a long way."

"Not in most of New York, but in subway miles, it will. But
what are you going to do for clothes? You'll need something
decent to wear to work."

"Or at least the interview," I chimed in.

"I guess your best bet is the hospital clothes room. You've
been there, right? Didn't you say they have a good collection?"

"They've certainly got a lot of clothes. I don't know how
appropriate the clothes are for work, though."

"Start there and we'll see what we need to do after that."

"Five minutes left of visiting time," a staff member called
out.

"Humphrey, I'm not planning on coming back. It's weird
to be on the other side, but I can't do this often. I hope you
understand."

"Are you kidding? I'm just happy you came once. It means a lot to me."

Gilda reached into her purse and opened her wallet. She pulled out a twenty-dollar bill and handed it over to me. "This will give you a little walking-around money."

"Thank you."

Gilda searched through her purse until she found a piece of scrap paper and a pen. "Here's my cell phone number. Call me when you get out, or anytime, for that matter. I've got the number here, so I'll check in."

"Thanks, Gilda."

"And stay strong. The worst part is behind you. Now you're moving on up."

"To the east side. To a deluxe apartment in the sky," I joked.

"Oh, Humphrey, you can always make me laugh."

18

I was meticulous in my hunt through the mountains of shirts and pants piled in the clothes room. I eventually found three solid button-downs and two plaid ones, which would be appropriate for a bookstore interview. Finding dress pants was also easy. But finding decent dress shoes was much more difficult. Going commando was a better option than wearing used underwear, and no one would be the wiser. But I needed socks; the light blue terry cloth hospital socks wouldn't be appropriate with anything but a hospital gown. Socks were available in a variety of colors, but I decided to spend a portion of Gilda's twenty dollars on new socks once I got out.

As the days dragged by, I found myself looking out the bedroom window more and more often. It had been early fall when I first arrived, and now the days had become much shorter, and I could predict when dinner would be called by how dark it was outside. The landscape had changed as well. In the past two months, I had watched as the leaves turned from green to yellow or red before eventually falling to the ground.

Sometimes the staff played DVDs like *Ace Ventura* or *Taxi Driver* in the evenings and on weekends, but I had been there so long I was seeing too many repeats of the limited selection. There was a wide variety of old magazines available, ranging from surfing magazines to *The New Yorker*, but in general the atmosphere didn't lend itself to reading.

The groups didn't do much for me either. The few I attended depressed the hell out of me. Sometimes the leader would speak of such elementary tasks as the value of eating fruits and vegetables or why it was important to wash your hands before meals. I spent much of the time observing the other patients as they listened to these sermons and wondering if it was possible that some of these people were hearing this information for the first time. Though I hadn't spoken to my family in over two years, at least I had been taught the basics like the proper way to hold a fork, unlike many of the patients who held it with a fist and shoveled the food into their mouths.

Patients came and went. Some were quiet and reserved; others entered like a human hurricane yelling and screaming until they received the needle. This always brought excitement to the ward; there was little else to look forward to. I became anxious and paced the hallways, keeping an eye on the staff, hoping to catch someone's eye just before they notified me of my discharge. There was an all-new batch of patients by then, and even Unknown was released before me.

All the while my mind never drifted far from Gilda. She made my stay bearable, as she called every few days, and I wondered if Wade was right. Was Gilda in love with me, or was she just being a good friend by helping someone endure the grind of institutional life? Though I was anxious about my future, I felt comforted with an angel looking out for me.

Finally on a Monday morning in the first week of January, Caroline approached me. "Are you ready to get out of here?"

"Like you wouldn't believe," I replied.

"Well, today's your lucky day. Gather your things. You only have three hours to get to the shelter, or else you may lose your bunk and get stuck spending the night in a drop-in center."

I leaped out of my chair and marched back to my room. Inside Mike and Noah were laughing their asses off.

"What's so funny?" I asked.

They both looked up at me and tried to catch their breath. "Mike called 911 and made a bomb threat," Noah said, giggling.

"Why in the hell did you do that?"

"Because it's funny," said Mike.

"You'll be lucky if they don't throw your ass out of here."

"You make that sound like a bad thing," said Mike.

"And you'll be lucky if they don't throw you in jail." I went to my closet and began shoving my clothes into a brown paper bag.

"They're not going to throw me in jail. Remember? I'm crazy." Mike raised his hand and gave Noah five.

"You never know. Making false bomb threats is a pretty serious offense."

"How are they going to prove it was me? Tell me that. How are they going to prove it was me?"

"Maybe I'll just tell them."

Mike's and Noah's faces dropped. "You wouldn't do that."

"I just might."

"Why would you do that?"

I shook my head and smiled. "Ah, hell. I'm not going to do that. I'm getting out of here."

"For real?" said Noah.

"You betcha."

"Congratulations." Mike got up and bumped my chest with his own. I wondered if I would miss these guys. Watching them had been one of my few amusements the last couple of weeks.

"How long have you been in here, Humphrey?" asked Noah.

"Two months."

"For real?" said Mike. "I've been in here a month, and it feels like a year," said Mike.

"Well, my friend, I'm here to tell you, it doesn't get any better."

Walking down the hallway looking at the open bedroom doors and the blank looks of the other patients, I thought about how I was never going to see these people again. Not that I would miss them, but I doubted that I would ever forget them.

Just as I sat down in a chair in the TV room to wait for my escort down to the property room, three police officers burst into the unit.

"What's the problem?" the on-duty staff member asked.

"A bomb threat came from the pay phone in this unit," said one of the police officers.

"I don't think there's a bomb in this unit," said the staff member.

"We don't either, but we've got to be sure."

By this time, patients were pouring out of their rooms to find out what was going on. Mike and Noah were among the last to appear.

"We need all of the patients out here so we can check their rooms and find out if this is a real bomb threat," said the police officer.

I buried my face in my hands. Just my luck that the moment I was getting out of this hellhole, those two jokers would call in a bomb threat. I considered ratting them out but decided against it.

Despite the seriousness of the matter, the police didn't show much urgency. The patients just stood around looking at each other with their arms crossed as the officers walked around the unit looking in the closets and under the beds and desks.

Someone turned off the television and the radio so that the only sounds were the squeaking of chairs being pushed across the floor as the staff member straightened up the unit. Everyone looked around, trying to determine who the culprit was. Finally the officers returned from the sleeping quarters.

"Anything?"

"No."

"I didn't think so."

The officer in charge now turned his attention to the patients. The staff and nurses stood to the side listening.

"I know whoever did this probably thought it would be a good joke," said one of the policemen, "but this is not a laughing matter. Given the state of the world, we have to take these things seriously. Calling in a bomb threat is a felony and is punishable with at least a year in jail. I don't know what you wanted to accomplish, but I can assure you, if it happens again, we will find out who is responsible. Do you understand?"

I looked over at Mike and Noah, who were trying to cover their laughter with their hands. I looked at the clock above the nurses' station. It was twelve o'clock. I had two hours to get to the shelter.

19

Outside the hospital the breeze hit my face for the first time in two months. It was cold. I wished I had taken some gloves from the clothes room at the hospital. I only had twenty dollars and a one-way subway ticket in my pocket. I was craving some junk food, and tempted by the smells coming from the hot dog stand camped out in front of the hospital, I immediately bought a two-dollar hot dog with mustard and ketchup. Though I wanted a soft drink as well, I restrained myself and slowly chewed each bite of the hotdog, savoring the flavor of the tasty treat.

When I was finished, I shoved my hands deep into my pockets and looked up and down First Avenue. I didn't have the faintest clue where the closest subway station was. Though time was an issue, I was not concerned. Manhattan was a small place. I was sure that I would come across one soon enough. But after walking several blocks and seeing no sign of a station, I asked a stranger.

"Grand Central is at Forty-second and Lexington. You should be able to get anywhere you want from there," said the stranger.

I peered down Third Avenue, saw a sign for Thirty-fifth Street, and knew I should walk in the other direction. Feeling better about things, I walked up Third Avenue and took a left and continued until I hit Lexington. I looked at the building on the northern corner. People flooded in and out the multiple doors. That must be the place.

As I looked around Grand Central Terminal, I was over-whelmed by the huge staircase at each end of the main room, and in the middle, an enormous, lighted board hanging high and displaying the departures and arrivals for the trains headed upstate, to Connecticut, and even to Canada. Every few min-utes the sign would click and the numbers and times and des-tinations changed. After a couple of minutes, I located the sign to the underground and took the escalator down to the subway.

I found a map. All I knew was the homeless shelter was at 180th Street and Eleventh Avenue. It took me several minutes to gather my bearings before I found which subway to take and which direction to go. I was going to have to make two trans-fers.

I slid my card and walked through the gate. I was to ride on the 4, 5, and 6, which confused me. Were they all going to the same place? As I walked through the station, I saw a sign on one side of the tracks reading "Express" and another on the other side reading "Local." *Well, I might as well get there as soon as possible, I thought.*

The express train pulled into the station. I was relieved the train was not crowded, and I could find a seat. I watched the monitor as the train moved uptown. Fifty-ninth Street, Eighty-sixth, 125th—I began to relax. I looked at all of the different passengers. A couple of times I made eye contact and quickly looked away. I focused my attention on the different advertisements just under the ceiling of the subway car.

I had been accustomed to taking the subway in Boston, but it was different in New York. With the empty soda bottles rolling around on the floor and abandoned newspapers in the seats, the New York subway felt dirty and unkempt. Coupled with the large variety of ethnic groups, I started to feel uncomfortable. A man with no legs entered the subway car using his arms as locomotion as he went by, singing, "I have no legs. I have no legs. I have no legs." At least I wasn't that guy. He would probably be happy to be at a homeless shelter if it meant he could have his legs back.

At 149th Street I transferred to the 2, which took me across town to the west side, before I changed trains one last time until I arrived at 181st Street. I headed west. I was expecting a sign on top of a door reading, FORT WELLINGTON MEN'S SHELTER, but there wasn't one, and I walked right past a group of men smoking cigarettes on the stairs in front of the entrance.

I circled the block because I was reluctant to ask for directions. But about halfway around, I realized the shelter was most likely where the men were smoking cigarettes, so I continued walking around the block until I came back to the building.

"Excuse me. Is this Fort Wellington Men's Shelter?" I addressed the group as a whole.

"Right through those doors, young man," a voice replied.

I walked up the steps and into the lobby, but it was nothing like a hotel. There were only two men sitting at a table with a clipboard in front of them. There was an iron gate like a street barricade at a parade. To the right stood a uniformed security guard watching an opening in the iron gate. I looked around.

Behind the desk was an extremely high ceiling like one in a high school gymnasium, but I didn't see any basketball goals, only rows and rows of beds.

"Can I help you?" asked the doorman.

"Is this Fort Wellington Men's Shelter?"

"Yes, can I help you?"

I cleared my throat. "I'm Arnold Humphrey. I'm coming from New York Community Hospital. I'm supposed to have a bed here."

The bearded black man flipped through the clipboard. "You said your name is Arnold Humphrey?"

"Yes."

"You barely made it here on time. It's one forty-five."

"You really keep time of when we're supposed to be here?"

"You bet we do. Two o'clock is our cutoff every day."

I looked around and wondered where everyone was. Caroline had told me there were over two hundred men at this shelter, but besides the men smoking cigarettes out front, the place was desolate.

Apparently the man could tell what I was thinking. "Residents can't stay in the shelter during the day except at lunch," said the man.

"Where am I supposed to go?"

"Anywhere but here. Sunday through Thursday you have to check back in by eleven at night. One in the morning on the weekends."

"That doesn't sound bad."

The man grunted. "Did you bring your meds?" he asked.

I reached into my bag and pulled out the two bottles.

"Hand them to me. Meds are given out at eight in the morning and six at night. You're responsible for taking your meds. We don't hunt you down. We've got enough things to worry about besides that."

I nodded.

"There's no smoking, drinking, or taking drugs in the facility. We can and will ask you to leave if you are caught. I don't have to tell you that you'll have limited options if you are forced to leave. Do you understand?"

"Yes, sir."

The man smiled. "You've never been in a place like this before, have you?"

"I just left the mental hospital." I didn't like the fact that the man was implying I wouldn't know how to handle myself.

"It's not the same. Trust me."

"I know that."

"Best keep your valuables on you at all times until you get a lock for your locker."

"Locker?"

"This building used to be a high school. Everyone gets a locker to store his valuables. What's in the bag?"

"Clothes."

"Pretty boy like you probably has some pretty nice duds, and believe me, if anyone sees something they like, they will take it. Right off your back, if you don't watch yourself. You got the hang of things?" he asked, but he didn't wait for a response. "Let me take you to your bunk."

The man led me past the security guard and through the gate. On the other side were the bunks lined up straight like a well-planted cornfield. As I walked between the beds, I smelled the old familiar smell of sweaty socks and mildewed clothes. Finally we stopped in front of an unmade bed. Folded sheets and a small blanket lay on the end.

"We change the sheets once a week," said the man.

"What day is that?"

"Monday."

I began to unfold the sheets.

"There will be plenty of time to do that later. Like I said, you can't be in the bunkhouse during the daylight hours."

"What time is dinner served?"

"Five o'clock people start lining up outside. You'll see. Just follow the others, and you'll be all right. Any other questions?"

"Where are the phones?"

The man pointed to the far corner of the room, where there were six pay phones. "You can't use them until after five o'clock."

"What time is it?"

"Probably around two fifteen or two thirty. Follow me. I'll take you back to the front, and you can be on your way."

We walked back through the sea of beds and past the security guard, who watched but didn't say anything. I stopped in front of the desk and waited for last-second instructions.

"That's orientation, son. It's not much. I hope you like it here."

20

I turned around and walked through the glass door and outside, where the same group of men was smoking cigarettes. Actually, I couldn't tell if it was the same men or if it was a different group doing the same thing. I didn't care. I wasn't planning on socializing very much. Though I supposed the shelter was better than the hospital, I still needed to get the hell out of there as soon as possible.

Having been locked up for two months, I took advantage of my freedom and started to walk. This was as much out of the need to get some exercise as it was out of the need to stay warm. It almost seemed like cruel and unusual punishment to make the residents stay outside all day, but I supposed it was the best way to motivate them to find a job. Surely working was better than this.

I needed a goal—at least a short-term one. I decided I would take this time to find some socks and a lock. I hoped I had enough money. I was looking for a good deal. I wasn't planning on blowing my remaining eighteen dollars on some argyle socks. All I wanted were some dark socks with enough elastic to last until I got a paycheck.

I hit pay dirt when I saw a street vendor selling socks, books, sunglasses, toboggans, and a menagerie of everything else under the sun. I picked up the socks. Rather than being fluffy socks, they were thin but with tight elastic. There was a handwritten sign that read, SOCKS $2.00.

"How about I give you five dollars for four pairs?" I called out.

"How about you give me five dollars for three pairs?" the vendor replied.

"Six dollars for four pairs?"

The man scratched his forehead and looked around to see if anyone was listening. "That's a deal."

I handed over my six dollars and picked up the four pairs of socks. "Got a bag?"

The man looked up at me like he should charge me another dollar for the luxury, but he opened a black plastic bag and slid the socks inside before handing it back to me. "You sure you don't need some gloves, too? It's cold out here. I'd hate to see you catch pneumonia because you didn't have a pair of gloves."

"I've got deep pockets."

"That's what I like to hear. So, do you need some gloves? The winter is still in front of us."

"That's all right." I kept the remaining twelve dollars.

I supposed it was approaching five o'clock, so I went to a locksmith looking for a combination lock but had to settle for a cheaper one with a key that cost nine dollars. I only had three dollars left. Not even enough for a keychain. I needed that money to call Gilda. I headed back toward the shelter. The day hadn't been too bad, but I was seasoned enough to realize that the jubilation of being free from the hospital would lessen. Day after day of battling the elements was going to get old.

When I approached the shelter, a long line had already formed leading up to the front door. Would it be that much trouble to allow us inside the building rather than let everyone freeze like ice cubes?

"What time is it?" I asked the man in front of me, who was wearing a watch.

"Don't know."

"Look at your watch."

"Doesn't work," replied the man with a shake of his head.

"It's about four forty-five," another voice called out.

"Do they ever let us in early?" I asked.

"Better chance of late than early," replied the man.

"What do they usually have?"

"It ain't Mama's home cooking. That's for sure. But if you're like the rest of us, you'll eat about plain anything."

"I heard that," another voice called out. "What you don't eat, you can give to me."

Dinner was called. A murmur of expectation rippled through the residents as we moved toward the door with as many people slipping indoors as possible. Unlike in the hospital where everyone was served the same food, at the shelter the resident walked through the line and chose what he wanted. Each server spooned the food onto a plate before handing it to the next server. At the end of the line, a server handed the plate to the resident. I chose fried chicken, green beans, salad, mashed potatoes, and iced tea.

I looked around the room and felt the same way I had the first day at the hospital. Only this time there were about ten times as many people, and it was about ten times as loud. Everyone was rejuvenated from being indoors.

I looked for an empty table, but I was far enough back in the line that every table had at least one person already sitting there. I sat beside an old black man wearing a gray warm-up suit with the hood pulled over his head. He looked up at me when I sat down.

"How you doing?" I asked.

"I'm Muhammad Ali. I'm in training to fight the great George Foreman. No one thinks I can win. They say Foreman is too strong. They say I am too old. But they don't know or have forgotten one thing about me. I have heart, and I have brains." He threw several quick punches in the air and completed the exchange with a big right uppercut.

"Good luck, champ," I said. "My money is on you. I know you can do it."

"I don't care what you think. If George Foreman was sitting in the same place as me, you would tell him the same thing."

"Doubt it."

"It doesn't matter what you believe. The Honorable Elijah Muhammad will guide me to victory. With him on my side, I can't be beat."

Another man sat down at the table. He looked at Muhammad Ali and smiled. "Who are you fighting this week? Joe Frazier again?"

"He's fighting George Foreman," I replied.

"Don't talk for me, little white man. I can talk for myself. The days of the white man speaking for the black man are over. In case you didn't know, there is a black man in the White House."

"I did know that. In fact, I voted for him."

The other man said, "You'll have to excuse Muhammad. He's under a lot of pressure right now. You know, with the big fight coming up and all." He gave me a wink.

"I understand."

"Name's Larry."

"I go by Humphrey."

Larry was an older man, skinny as a beanstalk with brown hair down to his shoulders and parted down the middle. He kind of looked like Neil Young.

"I see that you still have your bag with you. Are you new, or are you smart enough to realize that if a thief wants it bad enough, he'll get it one way or the other?" asked Larry.

"Just got here today."

"Where you coming from?" asked Larry.

I hesitated.

"That's okay. You don't have to tell me. I understand."

"It's not that…"

"Trust me. It's okay. I know. First day out of the hospital is nerve-racking."

I looked up. "How did you know I was in the hospital?"

"Didn't they tell you? Everyone here is mentally ill. This is where they store us."

I took a bite of the fried chicken. I didn't know how I felt about living in the free world with a bunch of unsupervised loons. "Everyone?"

"Have to be. That's the main criteria."

"What's the matter with you?"

"Me? I'm schizophrenic. You?"

"Bipolar."

"Most of us are either schizophrenic or that vague label known as personality disorder. Stay away from them. They might be nice for a while, but they'll bite your ass in the end," said Larry.

"How can you tell the difference?"

"They're the ones trying to be your friends. That's how."

I looked hard at Larry.

"Not me. I know you're the new guy. I'm just trying to help you out. You can trust me."

I stood up with my tray. I didn't want to get tangled up with anyone, especially a con artist. Although Larry wasn't finished with his meal, he threw his napkin on his tray and followed right on my heels. *So this is how a personality disorder acts*, I thought. I dumped my plastic utensils and paper plate in the trash and hurried toward the bunk area.

"What's your problem?" Larry called out.

I stopped. "Listen. I'm sorry. I'm not looking to make friends. I'm looking to get the hell out of here with as few problems as possible."

"You just wait and see how good of a friend I can be to you," said Larry. "Now where's your bed?"

"Over there," I said, vaguely.

"I mean what street?"

"Street?"

"This is what I'm talking about. Don't you know that the rows and columns are divided up into streets and avenues? Just like the grid of Manhattan. So, what street are you on?"

"I don't know."

"Lead me to your bed, and I'll show you."

I relented. Maybe I did need someone to show me the ropes. I led Larry past the rec room where there were a dozen chess- and checkerboards and past the bathrooms until we reached the bunk area. I walked through the middle of the room, not exactly sure which bed was mine. I zigzagged, looking for an empty bed with sheets folded at the bottom of it, but I couldn't find the right one.

"This is why you need me. If you knew your street address, you wouldn't have this problem."

Finally I stopped at a bed I was fairly certain was mine. Larry began counting the rows to determine the streets. "You're at Twelfth Street and Eighth Avenue. You won't get lost next time."

I set my brown paper bag on the bed and sat next to it. "Thanks."

"No problem. You are going to lock those things up, aren't you?"

"Yeah. Give me a minute."

"That's fine. I've got time. Believe me. If anything, I've got time." Larry laughed and reached into his pants pocket and pulled out a pack of Cheyenne cigarettes. "Do you smoke?"

"No."

"We can go outside. I like a cigarette after a good meal," said Larry.

I stood up. "I need to get off some cables." I hoped a graceful exit like that one would rid me of Larry.

"Rule number one," said Larry with his right index finger wagging. "You never go to the bathroom alone."

"Why is that?"

"That's where the crackheads hang out. They'll jump your ass for a nickel." Larry raised his eyebrows.

"That's good to know."

"Have you been to the bathroom yet?" asked Larry.

"No."

"The first thing you'll notice is that the stalls don't have doors. The reason is so that it will hopefully keep the crackheads from smoking up in there, but it doesn't do much good. There's nothing you can do to slow a crackhead."

"I wouldn't know."

"Do you still need to go to the bathroom?"

"I guess I better, while I have an escort."

"Are you starting to get the picture? The good guys need to stick together so that the bad guys don't eat us up."

I bit my lip and looked around the room at all the creepy people. Finally I just shook my head. "I'm sorry, man. I'm just a little bit scared."

"That's all right. If you weren't scared, you wouldn't be having fun." Larry once again smiled, and then we shook hands. "We have to be careful. Their evil is stronger than our good."

21

In the evening I rode the subway down to Gilda's apartment at Seventy-second Street on the Upper East Side. I was a little nervous. When I buzzed the apartment from downstairs, I wasn't sure what would be the appropriate way to greet her. With a hug? With a kiss? With a hug and a kiss? None of the above? Fortunately Gilda felt none of these inhibitions. She practically jumped into my arms and kissed me on the neck, sending a tingle up my spine.

"Come in. Come in," said Gilda, backing away. "You look good in your new clothes. You really hit the jackpot, didn't you?"

"It certainly beats the light blue hospital pajamas."

"How does it feel to be out?"

"Like I'm seeing things in color for the first time."

Gilda led me into her one-bedroom apartment. Empty Diet Coke cans were scattered around the room, and an ashtray overflowed with cigarettes. I guessed she felt comfortable enough with me not to tidy up.

"Sit down. Tell me about the homeless shelter. Do you want anything to drink?" Gilda was moving around a mile a minute and talking nonstop. I had never seen her so speedy and wondered if she was taking her medication.

"I'm fine," I said.

"A beer or wine?" Gilda called from the kitchen.

"Maybe just one beer."

The refrigerator opened and closed. Gilda returned a moment later with a bottle in each hand.

"So, how is the homeless shelter? Surely it's a nice change from the hospital," said Gilda.

"Actually, the hospital was much better. If you thought privacy was an issue at the hospital, try sleeping in a gymnasium with two hundred other people."

"It's that bad, huh?"

Gilda never took her eyes off me. She was obviously happy to see me, and her attention was intense, and I felt nervous. To break the spell, I stood up and walked around, studying photographs of friends in cute little frames spread across the room. There were guys in a couple of the pictures, but none looked like a boyfriend.

"Have you had time to read *Venus in Furs*?" asked Gilda.

I turned around to face her. She threw her head back for the last sip of beer, stood up, and headed for the kitchen.

"That's a fucked up book," I said.

"Would you like another beer?" Gilda called out from the kitchen.

"Not yet."

"But could you relate to it? I mean, did you get it?" Gilda asked, returning to the living room but not sitting. Instead, she stood about five feet away from me with her wild blue eyes surging with energy.

"It was hard for me to relate to it," I said.

"Not even the least bit?"

"Not really. I couldn't understand being a slave to a woman who wanted nothing to do with you sexually or who even respected you, for that matter, but only wanted to torture you. I can't imagine succumbing to that."

"Well, of course Masoch was exaggerating to get his point across, but did you get it, is my question."

"I guess so," I replied, hesitantly.

"You've never acted like that with a girl?"

"A little clingy maybe, but I never acted that needy. Why? Have guys acted like that with you?"

"No, I've acted that way with them. Throwing myself at guys who didn't want to have anything to do with me."

"You're too pretty for that to happen often."

"You don't know."

"Gilda, we've all made fools of ourselves. It doesn't mean we can't change. I stole a lot of money from my parents. That doesn't mean I'm going to steal from you."

"But it's your history. You can't change that past."

"That's why you're the crazy girl."

"Don't say that. I've got a complex about it." Gilda bit her lip and stared at me. "Can I ask you something, Humphrey?"

"Sure."

"Have you ever been in love?"

"If you're asking have I ever let a woman walk all over me, the answer is no, I have not."

"Not even a little bit?"

"No."

"Hmm. I guess the book didn't make much sense to you."

"Not really."

I finished my beer. Without saying anything, I placed the bottle on the coffee table and leaned back on the couch.

"Would you like another?" asked Gilda.

"Does a one-legged duck swim in circles?"

She smiled. "Well, you initially said just one."

"So this time I'll say this is my last one. Eventually I'll be right."

Gilda got another beer.

"I do have to be back at the shelter by eleven. There is no room for error on that." I was fishing for an invitation to spend the night even if it meant sleeping on her couch. Even if it meant sleeping on the floor, for that matter. But Gilda didn't bite.

"Every night?"

"One o'clock on the weekends."

"That's not so bad. I hope you don't mind, but I've invited my sister and her boyfriend over."

"Why would I mind?"

"I don't know. But if they ask how we know each other, just say we're in a writing group together."

"I don't want to lie," I said.

"Just until they get to know you. I don't want to throw up any red flags."

"Which reminds me," I said. "Have you had a chance to speak with your boss about me coming to work at Barnes & Noble?"

"I did mention it. In fact, I brought home an application so you can fill it out and return it to the store at Eighty-sixth and Lexington."

"There's one more little thing," I said in a higher-pitched voice. "Could I borrow twenty more dollars? I had to spend the other twenty on a couple of things, and I don't even have

enough money for subway fare home tonight. I could panhandle—"

"Stop. I'm not going to let you panhandle." Gilda walked
back to her bedroom and returned with both a twenty-dollar
bill and the application. "Here," she said, "and don't even think
about thanking me. It is my pleasure."

"Gilda, you are a good friend. I feel bad for the people who
have no one to help them out. I couldn't do this without you."

"Don't feel too bad for those people. They most likely
burned those bridges of their own accord."

"I have burned bridges. In fact, lots."

"And I'm here to help you rebuild them."

Gilda and I spent the next hour talking. I had worried we
wouldn't have anything to talk about after leaving the hospital,
but as she joked, "You can ask a writer anything, and they'll give
you an answer whether they know anything about the subject
or not."

The conversation never slowed until the buzzer sounded at
half past seven.

"That must be my sister and her boyfriend. I think you'll
like them. They are absolute hoots."

"They don't know you were in the hospital?"

"They know. I just don't want them to know you were,
too."

"Why not?"

"They might question my judgment. Or even worse, they
might judge you."

Gilda stood by the doorway and waited for her sister and
her boyfriend to tramp up the stairs to the fourth floor. The
two sisters greeted each other with high-pitched shrieks, and
then a young man entered the room with a sheepish look on his
face when he saw me. He was a handsome man with dark skin,

broad shoulders, short wavy hair, and a strong chin. I shook his hand and introduced myself.

"George King," he said.

"And this is my sister, Regina," said Gilda.

I gently shook Regina's bony hand. She was shorter and thinner than Gilda. She also wore more makeup, but she didn't need to. With her high cheekbones and voluptuous lips, Regina was a natural beauty.

After introductions, Regina spoke up. "Can a girl get a drink around here?"

Gilda turned to me. "First thing you need to know about my sister. She's a functioning alcoholic."

"That's a hell of a thing to say about a person. Maybe I just want a club soda," said Regina, though it was obvious she was taking the statement as a joke.

"The only way you would drink a club soda is if it was mixed with scotch," said Gilda.

"That may be true, but you don't need to be so blunt about it."

I finally got a word in edgewise. "I need another beer as well."

"Yeah, I think Humphrey may be a functioning alcoholic as well," said Gilda.

"I don't know about functioning," I replied, and the moment passed as everyone walked into the living room. Regina took a seat on the couch, while George and I sat in chairs.

"What do you do for work?" asked George.

"Unemployed. But Gilda is trying to hook me up."

"At the bookstore?"

"Like I said, I don't know if you could consider me functioning," I replied.

Gilda returned with three beers in her hand. I always liked it when girls drank beer. Despite their beauty, it made me believe these girls were not so vain. Gilda played a Jack Johnson CD, and everyone but me smoked a cigarette.

"So I understand you met Gilda in her writing group," said George.

I looked over at Gilda, who was enthralled in an animated conversation with her sister. I wished she had given me more notice about the fabrication. I didn't know the first thing about how a writing group worked.

"Yes. I just joined," I said.

"Do you mind me asking what your genre is?" asked George.

"Literary fiction."

"Really? That's great. Who are some of your influences?"

I smiled. George was a good guy. "I don't know exactly who my influences are, but my favorite writer is Kerouac."

"That's great. Regina and I just returned from San Francisco. We went to City Lights bookstore where Kerouac, Ginsberg, Ferlinghetti, and the other beats hung out. It was cool."

"I've heard of it."

"Never been to San Francisco?" asked George.

"Never."

"That's a shame. Everyone should go there. It's like the mistress to New York City."

"It's on the top of my wish list."

George turned to Gilda. "You mind if I bum one of those cigarettes?"

"Of course not. Don't even ask." Gilda handed the pack over to him, and I watched him light the cigarette and inhale.

"Where are you from, George?"

"Oh yeah. George is a suburbanite," said Gilda.

"Connecticut," said George.

"Land of the bulls and bears," I said.

George laughed and blew smoke out of his mouth. "I didn't grow up in Greenwich. A little further away in a suburb of Hartford, but actually I do work on Wall Street."

"Who with?" I asked.

"Who did I start with? Or who do I work for now?"

"I guess that's a genuine question in today's market," I said.

"I started with Merrill Lynch, but now I work for Morgan Stanley Smith Barney."

I remained quiet. I knew little about stocks and bonds. George must have noticed my apprehension, because he let the conversation drop.

"Can I get another beer?" asked George.

Gilda held up her bottle and shook it. "Get me one too."

"Me three," I said. It was a tired old joke, and no one bothered to laugh.

George handed three beers around and grabbed the empty ones.

"Just put the bottles on the counter. I'll rinse them out later," said Gilda.

"I don't mind."

"What time is it?" I asked.

Gilda looked at her watch. "Eight o'clock. What time do you have to leave?"

"Around ten."

"You have plenty of time."

George returned from the kitchen.

"Where do you live, Humphrey?" asked George.

I cleared my throat. "Washington Heights."

"Washington Heights! Why the hell do you live all the way up there?"

"I'm just happy to live in Manhattan. A starving artist doesn't have a whole hell of a lot of options in New York City."

"But he's thinking about moving," said Gilda.

"Where do you live?" I asked.

"Right around the corner," Regina replied.

"If I get Humphrey a job at Barnes & Noble, then he can get an apartment in the area."

"Do you want to live on the Upper East Side, too?" asked Regina.

"That would be great."

George reached over and grabbed another cigarette. I guessed he only smoked when he drank, and then he smoked plenty. "You know, I've got to envy you two."

"And why is that, George?" asked Gilda.

"Chasing your dreams. Really going for it. I remember when I was in high school I always wanted to be a professional basketball player."

"Were you that good?" asked Regina.

"I was good, but not NBA good. But I was young, and I've always dreamed big. Then one day, I don't know exactly when, but I just kind of realized I wasn't going to make it, and I gave up. But those days when I did hope and dream were probably the happiest days of my life."

"Even more than now?" asked Regina.

George picked his words carefully. "It was different. Now I'm making tons of money, but my name isn't in lights like I hoped it would be. Sure, I might get a blurb in the *Wall Street Journal* one day, but I'm never going to be famous, and I'm certainly not doing anything to improve the world. Hell, after the financial breakdown, most of the country loathes what I do."

"I guess I had never thought of it that way," I said.

"George. Honey. You have enough money now where you could go off on your own and do anything you wanted and not worry about the money," said Regina.

"I can't play basketball again."

"But you could try something else."

"I don't have any other particular talents. Though I must admit, I have always wanted to be a sports commentator, but I think that's every man's dream. How about you, Humphrey? Wouldn't you like to call a football game?"

"Hell yes! But I've never thought I had the voice for it."

"You see! I don't have a voice for it either. You've got to have that God-given talent. It takes more than just wanting it."

Regina walked over to George and wrapped his head in her arms. "I'm sorry, George. I didn't mean to upset you." Regina winked at me.

George raised his head and smiled. "It's not that big of a deal. We all have to play our role in life. Mine's a hell of a lot better than most."

I thought about that last statement and realized it was exactly what I was thinking about my life. I was born this way, and there was little I could do about it but try to be a better man. I looked over at Gilda. She was beautiful, smart, and as far as I could tell, she was also a good person. If Gilda couldn't change my life, then no woman could.

After the group hug ended, we broke into conversations of two once again. I felt a little drunk and George looked about the same.

"You're a good sort, Humphrey," said George.

"I appreciate that. You're not too bad yourself."

George looked over at Gilda and Regina to make sure they weren't listening. "You know, Humphrey, I'm glad you and Gilda are together."

I broke in. "We're not a couple."

"Regardless. Like I said, you're a good sort, and Gilda needs a good man in her life. She usually hangs around assholes, and I should know. Ninety-nine percent of the people I work with are assholes."

"I'm sure it's not that bad."

"Listen, you be good to Gilda. I've known her for almost two years. You stay good to her, and you'll stay happy. I promise you that." George stood up. "Now let's get another beer. I want to get good and snookered."

And we did. I could not remember when I had a better time. Not that anything special happened. It was just good, comfortable conversation, and I felt funny having to leave at ten o'clock. I put off leaving until ten fifteen when I knew I had to leave or risk having to sleep on the streets.

I was hurting for an excuse. I couldn't use work. A dentist appointment sounded reasonable but not strong enough. Instead I said my mom was in town. No one would argue with that, and no one did. I made eye contact with Gilda after the farewells were made, and she followed me out to the hallway.

"I had fun," I said.

"Me too. Even if I did barely get a chance to talk with you after my sister and George arrived."

"George is a good guy."

"I know he is. And I also know how long it's been since you had a normal conversation with a guy. I didn't want to take that away from you."

"Thanks."

"But next time it's just me and you. Deal?"

"Deal."

Gilda leaned forward and kissed me on the cheek.

22

I arrived back at the shelter at 10:58, tired and drunk. I walked past the security guard and meandered through the army of beds, trying to find mine. Many of the men were already in bed with their white sheets pulled over their heads to shield their eyes from the light. A couple of guys sat at each end of a bed playing gin. *Why didn't Gilda invite me to stay? What was holding her back?* I didn't know. Maybe she was just as unsure as I was, or maybe she didn't want to invite me to stay the night after I had just met her sister.

Finally I found my bed at Twelfth Street and Eighth Avenue. The man sleeping next to me was already snoring. Under each leg of the man's bed were shoes. I wondered if this was to prevent squeaking. Pretty considerate. Then I looked around and saw that most of the residents had done the same thing.

"Why does everyone have their shoes under the legs of their beds?" I asked my neighbor.

"So they don't get stolen in the middle of the night."

Now in stocking feet, I realized I needed to use the bathroom and brush my teeth. *Damn I'm drunk.* I retrieved my shoes from under the bed and searched for Larry. I couldn't remember if Larry had told me where his bed was or if I had just forgotten. Not able to find him, I hustled over to the bathroom. There was a line for the toilets, but not a soul brushing his teeth. I turned on the water and squeezed the toothpaste on the brush.

"Hey, Waldo! What are you doing here?" called out a deep voice.

I was amused enough by the comment to turn my head and see who the voice was referring to. Foaming at the mouth from the toothpaste, I saw a brick house of a black man with yellow eyes and his three cronies staring at me. *Uh-oh. Larry was right. I should have come with an escort.* I tried to avoid the man by turning around and spitting the toothpaste into the sink. I looked in the cracked mirror to see if they were approaching. Not seeing them, I thought the danger had passed, but I still desperately needed to use the bathroom.

I placed my toothbrush on the sink and walked over to the urinal. Even with the nerves, it only took a second before I had a steady stream. Suddenly a hand grabbed my right shoulder.

"Waldo, I'm talking to you."

Trying to pull my shoulder free but still peeing, I turned around far enough that some pee squirted on the man's shoe and lower leg. My eyes bugged as I looked up and saw the man looking down. "What the hell are you doing, french fry?"

"I'm sorry. Are those your shoes?"

"Damn right, they're my shoes. Whose do you think they are? And you're going to clean it up. It's about time a white man shined my shoes rather than the other way around."

My flow had stopped.

"Kick his ass, Raymond," called out a shrill voice.

"You're lucky I don't take a hammer to your head and nail you to the floor."

"You say the word, Raymond, and I'll get your toolbox," someone from the peanut gallery said. Wicked laughter followed.

"What are you doing here, Waldo? You don't look like you belong," said Raymond.

"I just got here earlier today from New York Community Hospital."

"You know you have to pay the toll," Raymond said as he stepped closer to me.

"Toll?"

"Give me your wallet. I'm taking everything that's in it."

I gladly handed over my wallet, knowing I had hidden the twenty-dollar bill Gilda had given me in my right shoe.

"Nothing?"

"I'm here for the same reasons you are. I'm broke."

Raymond threw the wallet back at me. "Get your white ass out of here and hold the rest of that pee for the night. And be happy about it."

I zipped up my pants and walked out of the bathroom, arriving back at my bunk before realizing I had forgotten my toothbrush. I guessed I would write that off.

By the time I had shed my shoes and placed them under the bedposts, four staff members were circling the room telling everyone to get to their beds.

"Lights out in five minutes! Get to your bunks."

The noise lessened as everyone did what they were told. I pulled the scratchy sheets over my tired body. A few minutes later, the lights were out.

Just as I was about to fall asleep, a voice called out, "Good night, John-Boy."

There were a few giggles.

"Good night, Tyrone."

More giggles.

"Good night, Earvin."

This was followed by several shushes, and angry grumblings echoed through the room as pillows were turned over and people squirmed in their sheets. Finally, just as it became quiet, someone laid a terrific fart. Everyone including me laughed.

At seven the next morning, the lights turned on. When I opened my eyes, many men were already walking around the room. I guessed they'd had trouble sleeping and instead spent the night patrolling the shelter.

I needed to use the bathroom, and though the incident from the night before was fresh in my mind, I hoped things would be a little more relaxed in the morning, and I was right.

Then I walked to the dining hall like the rest of the drones and waited quietly as the line moved forward. Breakfast consisted of a choice of cereal, apple or orange juice, a roll, and a hard-boiled egg. I sat down at a table, and soon after, Larry sat down beside me.

"I guess the date didn't go too well since you're back here," he said.

"It wasn't a date." I peeled back the wrapping on the still-frozen butter.

"If a girl asks you over to her place, then it's a date."

"We had a good time. Her sister and her sister's boyfriend came over. We drank a few beers and hung out. All in all it went well enough that she said she wanted to see me again."

"Sounds like she's a nice girl."

"Hopefully she's hooking me up with a job. I need to find a place of my own and get the hell out of here."

"How do you plan on doing that?" asked Larry.

"With money."

Larry laughed. "You can't get a place to live without a bank account."

"Then I'll open a bank account."

"You can't open a bank account without a power bill with your mailing address on it, and you can't receive mail at the shelter." Larry smiled.

"Then what the hell am I supposed to do?"

"Stay here. That's all you can do."

"How do the rest of these people get by?"

"Either on welfare or SSI."

"But where do they pick their checks up if they don't have a mailing address?"

"General delivery at the main post office down on Thirty-third Street. They start lining up on the last day of the month waiting to get their check. There's so many people it's usually not until the third day of the month before everyone gets their money."

"Where do they sleep?"

"On the sidewalk."

"What the hell!"

"They've got nothing else to do. It's like a big party. Then they go blow it all on lottery tickets until the next month rolls around," said Larry.

"Do you do that?"

"No, no." Larry shook his head emphatically.

"What do you do?"

"I get my check sent to a church I attend. They hold it for me. It sure beats waiting in line for three days."

"That's smart."

"Yeah, going to church is smart. You should go with me this Sunday."

"We'll see."

After breakfast Larry and I walked back to the bunk room. I planned on filling out my job application and going by Barnes & Noble that day. When we rounded the corner, several policemen were gathered around one of the beds. Many of the residents stood around on their tiptoes, looking over shoulders and trying to see what was going on. Others went so far as to stand on beds.

"Must be a drug bust," I said to Larry.

"Maybe. But then again, why would the paramedics be here?"

I looked closer and saw three paramedics behind the policemen. Upon closer inspection, I saw a gurney.

"I think he's dead," a voice finally said.

Everyone became quiet.

"Who is it?" asked Larry.

"I don't know. I think it's that old man who only eats bread and milk. I think he's been trying to malnourish himself," said the man.

"If he was, it worked," said Larry.

More people gathered.

"It's this nasty food we have to eat. Finally it's killed someone. Maybe they'll change now, but I doubt it," someone else said.

"It's lucky someone found him and called an ambulance. It wouldn't have surprised me if they just let him sit there and rot until he stunk."

"Probably won't even dig the full six feet."

"Yeah, not even enough for a curious dog."

"What about the coffin? Think they'll just wrap him in a blanket?"

"Are you kidding? A sheet at best."

"Move to the side, people," called out a police officer while the two others pressed forward to make an alleyway for the body to be carried through. Everyone's head dropped in respect, and no one said a word as two men pushed the gurney with a white sheet draped over the body.

I looked at Larry. With his eyes cast downward, he looked especially distraught.

"You all right, Lar? Did you know him or something?"

He looked into my eyes and said, "I don't want to die here."

"You won't. Didn't you say they were going to find you Section Eight housing? You'll be home free."

"That could be six months from now. I'm getting old. I might die here and be hauled away in a body bag like a casualty of war."

"Keep your head up. You'll be all right."

"I'm going outside to smoke a cigarette."

I walked away thinking about the dead man. I needed to get out of there. I needed a place to live.

23

I made up my bed neatly, tucking the sheets in and pushing all the wrinkles out so that it was as smooth as glass. I pulled a pen out of my pocket and filled out the job application. I hadn't asked Gilda if I could use her address or telephone number on the application, but I did it anyway. I wasn't about to admit to my future employer that I lived in a homeless shelter. When it came to past work experience, I said that I worked retail at Foot Locker and Banana Republic.

After breakfast everyone lined up for medication at three windows. As I waited, I wondered how many residents didn't take their medication out of the sheer inconvenience of the process. It took an hour. Afterward I lined up to take a shower in a single room with eight showerheads and another long line with guys covering their genitals with a tiny white towel barely large enough to wrap around even the skinniest guy's waist.

"You're smart having flip-flops," one of the residents said to me.

I looked around. About half of the people wore sandals of some kind. "No telling what kind of fungus a person could catch in a shower with two hundred people," I said.

"Where did you get them?"

"At the hospital," I replied, not even looking over at the guy, hoping the conversation would soon end.

"You think I could borrow them some time?" he asked.

I finally looked at the man. He had a huge head with a beard and feet that looked to be about a size fourteen with nails that looked like a bird's talons. "I don't think they would fit," I said.

"Not to walk around in, but for the shower they would be okay."

"If I let you wear them, it kind of defeats the purpose. No offense, but I don't know what kind of disease you may have on your feet."

"Be like that then."

I showered and walked back to my bed. It was just after nine o'clock. Everyone would have to clear out by ten. Barnes & Noble opened at ten as well. I wanted to arrive early, before it got busy, so I'd have a better chance of meeting the manager.

I put on my plaid button-down and khaki pants. I was a little nervous about going to the bathroom by myself but even more embarrassed to ask a stranger to escort me to the bathroom like I was a girl on a bad date, so I braved the trip alone. After brushing my teeth and hair, I walked back out to the bunk room.

"Hey, Reverend! You going to a wedding or a funeral?" asked an older man, an ugly fellow with black hair greased back and his jaw sliding and shifting in every direction because he had no teeth.

"What?" I asked.

"What are you so dressed up for?" asked the man with his gummy smile.

I looked down. *What the hell kind of wedding or funeral does this joker go to if he thinks this is appropriate dress?* "I'm going on a job interview," I finally said.

"Why?"

"To make money."

"How much does the job pay?"

"Around nine dollars an hour, I think."

"You won't be able to get your check if you have a job."

"I don't want to be on SSI or welfare. I want to earn my money so I can get out of here."

"Ah hell. That ain't worth it. I probably make more money than that doing nothing."

"Hopefully I won't be making nine dollars an hour forever."

"Huh-uh. Sorry. Not for me. I'll just keep getting that Obama money." The man smacked his gums together and walked away.

I arrived at Barnes & Noble shortly after ten. I didn't have to look far to find Gilda. She was smiling and talking to a customer right up front. The twinkle in her eye said she enjoyed her work. I hoped I would too.

Still talking to a customer when I walked up, Gilda smiled even more when she saw me. In the meantime, I made myself busy by browsing through the magazines by the cash registers, picking up a *People* magazine.

"Hey, eager beaver," Gilda said as soon as her customer walked away.

She got better looking every time I saw her. Granted, I had only seen her twice since she left the hospital, where no makeup was allowed. I wondered if she was becoming more physically attractive or if my feelings for her had grown fonder.

"Anything to get away from that shelter. Someone died this morning or last night. He was discovered this morning."

"You're kidding."

"Honest to God."

Gilda's eyes narrowed. "Are you all right?"

"I'm fine."

"Did you know him?"

"I don't even know if I had ever even laid eyes on the man. This morning I only saw him after they put a white sheet over his corpse."

"That's terrible."

"Like I said, that's why I'm here. I probably would have been here anyway, but that removed all doubt."

"Let me take your application over to Brian. Maybe he has time to see you right now."

Bored with the magazines, I looked at the classic fiction, which had a shelf to itself. I never liked nineteenth-century writers like the Brontes or Thoreau. Too long-winded. Jane Austen was all right, I supposed, though I had only read *Sense and Sensibility*. I guessed a book had to be in print for a hundred years before it could be considered a classic. Why else wouldn't there be Fitzgerald, Hemingway, or Steinbeck on these shelves?

Gilda returned without the application. "Brian can see you now." She hooked her arm with mine and walked me through the store. "Don't be nervous. It's no big deal."

"It's a big deal to me."

"All right, maybe it is. Just don't let the bad morning at the shelter get you down. Be positive."

Gilda pushed open a door marked with a sign that read EM-PLOYEES ONLY and led me down a short hallway until we reached the manager's office. She pointed at the door and said, "Good luck."

I knocked twice on the open door. The manager looked up with a smile on his face. "Come in, Arnold."

I winced. I wondered how long it would take to tell him that I preferred to go by Humphrey.

"Sit down."

I had already forgotten the manager's name. I needed to listen for it. I couldn't count how many times I had been introduced to someone and forgotten his name two seconds later because I was too nervous to concentrate.

"My name is Brian Greene."

We shook hands. Brian walked back to his desk, sat down in his chair, and leaned back.

"So you're from Boston, Arnold."

"Yes, sir."

"I went to school at U Mass."

"Really? That's a good school."

"Yes. I enjoyed it very much. Maybe a little too much," he said with a laugh.

I didn't say anything.

"Why didn't you go to college?"

"I did for a little while. I just didn't finish."

"What were you studying?"

"That's why I quit. At the time I didn't know what I wanted to be. I always planned on going back."

"What do you want to be now?"

"I want to work at Barnes & Noble."

Brian smiled. "That's a good answer. Are you a big reader?"

"Yes, sir."

"What was the last thing you read?"

"*Venus in Furs* by Masoch," I replied.

"Hmm. I haven't heard of that one. Any good?"

"Kind of strange."

"Anyway, you don't have to be a big reader to work at Barnes & Noble. I'm sure that some of our employees read very little, but I do expect you to be courteous and try to answer the customers' questions the best you can. However, if you do read books, as an employee, you get forty percent off everything in the store."

I thought for a minute. "Does that mean I'm hired?"

"Yes."

"Right now?"

"Gilda speaks highly of you. That's a strong recommendation. We try to use referrals as much as possible. It seems to work best that way."

"When do I start?"

"Be here Thursday at nine thirty. We'll do some paperwork and start training you."

24

I could not stop smiling when I left Brian's office, and Gilda read the expression on my face from across the store. Without restraint she swooped across the room and hugged me long and hard.

"That was quick," said Gilda.

"It was all you. He said your recommendation was good enough for him."

Gilda and I stood about a foot apart. Normally I didn't like to be crowded and need a comfortable amount of space between the person I was talking to, but with Gilda, I didn't care. In fact, the only reason I noticed was to realize I didn't care. I looked at her pink lips and wanted to kiss them, but it wasn't the right time or place. There would be time for that later, I hoped.

"When do you start?" asked Gilda.

"Thursday."

"Oh my gosh. We've got to celebrate."

"Definitely."

"What should we do?" asked Gilda.

"I don't know. What time do you get off?"

"Five o'clock."

"Sounds like dinner then," I said.

"I wish I could leave now. What are you going to do with the rest of your day?" asked Gilda.

"I'll figure out something."

"Maybe you should go to the library. At least you would be inside, and you could sit down."

"Where is it?"

"The main library is at Thirty-ninth and Fifth."

"Sounds as good as anything."

"Meet me here at five o'clock sharp. I'll see you then."

There was a moment between the two of us. We looked at each other to make sure we were on the same page, and I walked away satisfied. This was not just a friendship between two people. This was more, and I was elated.

Outside, the winter wind greeted me, and I zipped my coat up to my chin. The streets were crowded with people walking with their heads down as they braved the cold. Luckily the subway was less than a block away, at Eighty-sixth and Lexington. As I walked down the steps to the trains, I couldn't remember ever feeling so good. Even in my wildest dreams, I couldn't believe everything would work out this well.

The library proved to be a godsend. The only problem was that I was so manic I couldn't focus well enough to read any new material; I only made it a couple pages through *David Copperfield* and an equally short amount of time through *Studs Lonigan*.

I needed to read a book I'd read before so that I wouldn't have to pay too close attention. I settled on *The Catcher in the Rye* and sat at a table on the third floor for the next four hours, occasionally walking around looking at the library books.

At four thirty I shelved the book and headed back to Barnes & Noble. I wondered how Gilda paid New York City rent on nine dollars an hour. Her parents must subsidize her. Gilda was at the door when I arrived.

"Are you ready?" she asked.

"Better put on that coat. It's bitter outside."

As we walked down the street, we were surprisingly quiet. I supposed it was too cold and windy to have a normal conversation, but still, I had never known Gilda to be at a loss for words. I considered grabbing her hand. It made sense. Holding hands would have warmed us up, but I decided against it; holding hands is a girl's first move.

In the apartment Gilda took off her jacket and hung up mine as well. Although I wasn't bringing anything to the table besides myself, she liked me. After all, she gave me money and landed me a job. I couldn't even buy her dinner tonight unless we went to McDonald's, and that would be with her money.

"Want a beer?" asked Gilda.

"Thanks."

"What did you have in mind for dinner?" she asked as she walked into the kitchen. "I don't know. What do you want?"

"I could cook dinner." Gilda returned from the kitchen and handed me a beer.

"Stop." I had heard enough. I stood up and looked Gilda in the eye. "If anything, I should cook dinner for you. You've done everything for me. At least let me cook dinner."

"You cook?" Gilda said.

"I dabble."

"What are you going to cook?"

"Whatever you want. Only thing is, you'll have to pay. I'm sorry. I still don't have any money. But now that I've got a job, I can pay you back soon."

"That's all right. I like helping you out."

"Just the same, it's important to me. I've taken enough handouts in my life. It's time to take some fiscal responsibility."

"If you insist, I won't stop you."

We returned from the grocery store with chicken, mushrooms, red peppers, broccoli, orange juice, and honey. Gilda already had the rest of the spices and sauces necessary for me to make my specialty: honey-glazed stir-fry.

"I'll help," said Gilda.

"You won't let me do anything on my own, will you?"

"Not if I can help it."

I shook my head in disbelief. I had always heard that when the right person came along, I would know it. Even though I was sane enough to realize it was too early to make long-term plans, I couldn't help but think there was something different between Gilda and me than anything I had experienced before.

"I'll cook some rice and slice the mushrooms," said Gilda.

"Okay. I'll mix the sauce and cut the other vegetables."

Gilda put on a pink apron and started in on the mushrooms. "Who taught you to cook? Your mother?" asked Gilda.

"Hardly. My mom was like you. She wouldn't let me do anything. I had a roommate in college who showed me the basics, and I just kind of took it from there. But don't think I'm a master. I have about ten meals in my repertoire."

"I guess college wasn't a complete waste of time for you. Plenty of people get out of college still not knowing how to cook."

I poured vegetable oil into the wok and turned on the burner.

"Mushrooms are ready. What about everything else?" asked Gilda.

"Done."

Gilda handed me the cutting board, and I scraped the vegetables into the wok. "You stir, while I cut up the chicken," I said.

Gilda grabbed a spatula off a hanger beside the sink and stirred the vegetables around as they began to sizzle.

"How's the food at the shelter?"

"About like you'd expect."

"Worse than the hospital?"

"Much."

"That's not good."

"All right, take out the vegetables and place them on a plate. I'm going to cook the chicken now."

After the chicken changed from pink to tan, I stirred in the sauce.

"It smells divine," said Gilda.

"Hopefully it will taste divine, too." I mixed the vegetables back in the wok. "How's the rice?"

Gilda removed the lid. "Looks done to me."

"Excellent. I'm starving."

"I'll set the table. Wine good for dinner?" asked Gilda.

"Wine would be divine."

"I like that word, don't you?"

"Yes, it's divine."

"I'm sorry I asked," Gilda said with a chuckle.

I sat down for dinner and took a bite of the chicken without waiting on her.

"Humphrey, we've got to toast."

"I'm sorry." I set down my fork and raised my wineglass. "To what?" I asked, hoping Gilda would say something. I hated making toasts.

"To happiness," said Gilda.

"To happiness."

We clinked glasses.

After a couple silent minutes, Gilda looked up at me with bright, adoring eyes.

"What did you think the first time you saw me?" she asked in a soft, tender voice.

"That you were crazy," I answered without hesitation.

She laughed. "No, no. Before that."

"That you were funny."

Gilda smiled again. "I mean, what did you think the first time you laid eyes on me before I said anything?"

This time I smiled. "That you were beautiful."

There was silence between us. I was wondering what to say next. I wasn't going to speak first; I was afraid I would ruin this crucial moment.

"So, Humphrey, what's your next move?" Gilda asked.

"That's what I was just thinking about."

"I thought you might be. I know you're not happy at the shelter."

"Better than the streets."

"How long do you think you'll stay?"

I finished off my glass of wine, and Gilda poured me another.

"I'm not sure how long I'll stay at the shelter. Probably a long time. I have some things I have to figure out. Like how I'm going to rent an apartment without a bank account. I need a utility bill with my name on it before I can open one. I don't know how I'm gonna do that."

Gilda set down her wineglass and placed her fork across her plate. She looked right at me. "You can use my address."

"I hope you don't mind, but I already used your address on the Barnes & Noble application."

"No problem."

"I appreciate that, but I still need my name on a utility bill," I replied.

"We'll figure that out. I don't want you staying at that shelter anymore. A man died there this morning, for Chrissake. That's no place for someone who is restarting his life. That's a place for people who have given up."

"I don't have any other options right now."

"You have one."

I stopped eating and laid down my silverware. "Are you telling me I can live with you?"

"That is, if you want to."

I smiled. "Well, of course I want to. Are you kidding? I'll help with the rent and all that. Don't worry about me. I'll be a good roommate."

"I know you will."

Gilda stood up and filled my glass once again, finishing off the bottle. "Should we open another?"

"I don't think so. Being bipolar, you and I should be careful not to drink too much."

Gilda smiled. "It's nice to have someone looking out for me."

"Yes, it is."

We stared at each other across the table. "Sometimes life just keeps getting better and better," said Gilda.

"When are you going to show me something you wrote?" I asked.

"I want to read your essay. Supposedly you're finished. You tried to get yours published. I'm still working on mine," said Gilda.

"I threw mine in the trash."

"Really?"

"Yes."

Gilda stood up. "We need to toast to that moment. I know it had to be tough to realize all that stuff wasn't true."

"Well."

"Are you going to continue writing?" asked Gilda.

"I want to write a book about life in the mental hospital."

"That's not a bad idea. I could tell you some stories. If you think people were crazy at Community Hospital, you should go to Bellevue. That's headquarters for the crazies in the world."

"I wouldn't want to steal your stories."

"I guess you're right." She paused. "I know what. We can go to Ground Zero tomorrow. Have you been there?"

"Are you crazy? I was scared to death of that place when I was sick. I thought they'd kill me if I got close."

"Good. It will be like killing the demons in your head. It can be a fresh start. Did you know they're building some kind of Muslim headquarters just one block from the World Trade Center?"

"I hadn't heard that."

"It hasn't been in the news in a while. Tea Partiers going nuts, that kind of thing," said Gilda. "I think they should build a mosque there. Show them that we will overcome, that kind of thing. Not all Muslims are crazy."

I didn't answer for a moment. "You know, I wish I hadn't thrown away that manuscript. I think it would be amusing to many people to see how the insane mind works."

"I don't know. Your topic could be considered insensitive to the victims."

"There you go again," I exclaimed.

"What?"

"Constantly trying to help people. I wrote an entire book, and not once did I consider how hurt the victims would feel."

"I suppose that's part of the illness. You get so focused on one thing that you can't even think of anything else."

"How about you?"

"For me it was my weight for the longest time. I battled anorexia in high school. Big into it. Was part of this cult that said they were 'pro-ana.'"

"What does that mean?"

"They promoted anorexia as a healthy lifestyle."

"Uhh."

"Messy stuff. Got that somewhat under control, and then had my first psychotic episode my sophomore year of college. Been battling it ever since. I can't seem to catch a break."

"I know how that is, but you just gave me a break."

Gilda's eyes were red. I walked over and put my arms around her waist. "You're not going to hurt me, are you?" she asked, sniffling.

"Oh, Gilda. I don't think so. No matter what happens, I'll always have the good memories of you taking care of me. I'm serious; you should be a doctor or something."

"I've considered going into social work. I think I would enjoy giving a voice to those that don't typically have one."

"I think you would be good at that. Where would you go to school?"

"I've been thinking about that. Maybe NYU."

"You'd stay in the city?"

"Makes sense. Family's close."

"That's a lot different from going to Iowa."

"I've had that experience. Now I appreciate how much New York has to offer. You can be anything you want in New York."

"At a price."

"I guess that is true." She looked down. "What you need to do is make amends with your family."

"That requires money."

"Let me put it this way. I don't know if I want to be friends with someone who has eliminated his parents from his life."

"Why is that?"

"If you'll give up on your parents, you'll probably someday give up on me."

I remained quiet as I processed what Gilda had just said. "You don't know my parents."

"No, I don't, but I guarantee they'll forgive you," continued Gilda.

"Maybe. Let me get settled first. It's hard knowing I stole from them."

"Don't be so hard on yourself. I'm sure it's not the first time it's been done."

"Great, now it's a copycat crime, too."

"You need to think of the present. You are missing time spent with them right now."

"Where's your phone? I'll call them right now if you want."

Gilda looked at her watch. "It's ten o'clock. Too late to be mixing those kinds of emotions. Let it settle until tomorrow, after we go to Ground Zero."

"I don't know how I feel about going," I said.

"Hopefully sad."

"I suppose that is how I'll feel."

"You look tired," said Gilda.

"I am."

"Let's go to bed."

"Okay." Of course, the big question was, where *was* I going to sleep? I had been thinking of this moment since she invited me to live there, but I wasn't planning on her telling me to hop in bed with her.

"I'm not going to make you sleep on the couch. What are you, my brother? I'll get you a blanket, just in case you get cold later tonight. I'm going to stay up a little longer. I'm wired."

I was completely confused by these mixed signals. I went to bed but didn't sleep for another hour. I listened to Gilda clean the kitchen and then turn on the TV. By the time I fell asleep, she still hadn't come to bed.

25

When I awoke in the morning, Gilda was looking at me. She looked a little unraveled with her hair pointing in all directions, but I'd seen her in much worse condition in the hospital. But I wasn't thinking of her hair, but rather her soft lips. I leaned forward and gently pecked them, not getting much effort out of Gilda. I pulled back slowly so I could judge her reaction.

"That was a surprise," she said as she wiped her mouth.

"Really?"

"You've never even flirted with me."

I pulled myself up in the bed. "What are you talking about? You didn't think I was flirting with you?"

Even Gilda seemed at a loss for words. "I guess that's a good thing. You probably don't cheat on your girlfriends," she said at last.

"Are you my girlfriend?"

"You move pretty quick," said Gilda.

"I didn't mean—"

"Easy. I'm pulling your leg."

"So was I. So we're even."

"Relax, Humphrey. I just want a nice guy. I'm a nice person. I'm done with mean guys. I don't understand them, and they don't understand me."

"What does that mean?"

"It means you're going to have to go through a series of tests to decide if you are dateworthy or just roommate material."

"You're kidding."

"Let's have a good day together. We're going to Ground Zero."

"You make it sound like it's party time."

"Well, it kind of is. You must not know about the Wall Street protestors gathering downtown. They've been down there for over a month."

"What's their beef?"

"They're mad at the richest one percent."

"Who are the protesters?"

"The poorest one percent."

"I can see why they don't like each other. They don't have much in common."

"Just got a job and already you're a snob," Gilda said.

"I am not. I've always looked down on the poorest one percent. There's no one else I can look down on."

"You're pretty peppy in the morning," said Gilda. "That's the kind of energy I expect out of someone who has been held in captivity for two months."

"I'm going to shower. I need to go back to the shelter and pick up my medicine and my clothes and check out of the place."

"Do that after we go to Ground Zero."

"You're certainly gung ho on this Ground Zero idea. You do know that I realize that it happened. That I was being absurd. I don't need it rubbed in my face."

Gilda clenched my hand. "It's not like that and you know it. Go shower while I set out breakfast. I say we leave here at ten. You can go uptown to the shelter in the afternoon. That'll get you out of the house for a while. Get rid of some of that aggression."

An hour and a half later, we were walking out of the City Hall subway station and over to the World Trade Center site. As we walked and she talked, I began to think she was more interested in seeing the Wall Street protestors than the World Trade Center Memorial. "The movement is spreading all over the world," she said enthusiastically.

"You're pretty hot on helping these hippies."

"Just because you don't like the messenger doesn't mean the message is wrong."

"I've got a job. I don't have time for that monkey business."

At Zuccotti Park we came across the protestors and their tents and blankets with the smell of incense drifting in the air. There was a scattering of signs claiming in some clever variation to be representing the "other 99 percent" as opposed to the nation's richest 1 percent who had something like 20 percent of the money.

I didn't know how I felt about it, except that I couldn't see this movement going much longer, with New York winter staring them in the face.

"What are they asking for?"

"Nothing. It's a silent protest," said Gilda.

We were standing at the corner of Liberty and Broadway when Gilda stopped walking. She looked at her watch and then looked at me.

"What are you waiting for?" I asked.

I looked over Gilda's shoulder and suddenly saw my parents walking toward me. I looked back at Gilda, and our eyes met.

"You had no right," I said, angry.

"I thought you said you were ready to call them," said Gilda and shrugged.

I looked over at my parents. My mom and I saw each other first. *Should I walk toward them or away?* I froze.

"Arnold," Mom said, but she stopped before touching me.

Mom, Dad, and Gilda all looked at each other. I realized this was the first time they had seen each other.

Gilda spoke. "I called them yesterday afternoon. I needed to make sure you were open to the idea."

"But I wanted to contact them on my own, Gilda."

"You certainly have a good friend in Gilda," Mom said. "She sent us a glowing report about your progress. I understand you went through some confusion and now you live in a homeless shelter."

I looked at Gilda.

"Trust me. This is the best way to start over. I've done it three times. You've got to have your family involved," said Gilda.

"I don't want to start over. I want to continue on the path that brought me here. I'm just going to watch where I step in the future."

"Don't worry about the money right now. We want to help you get on your feet," said Dad.

Before I argued, I stopped and took a deep breath. My parents were in my life. Their future role was unknown, but Gilda was right, they needed to be in it.

"Given my circumstances, I guess I can use as many people as possible in my corner," I said.

"You know something, Arnold," said Mom, "these past couple of years I've wondered if you had a mental illness. You changed a lot after you went off to college."

"I know. Once again, I'm sorry. On the plus side, I haven't felt this good in a long time, if ever."

"Are you going to stay at the shelter?" asked Mom.

"I'm moving in with Gilda."

"She told me you got a job at Barnes & Noble. So you want to stay in New York?"

I looked over at Gilda. A smile crossed her face, and our eyes met. "Yes, I think I do," I replied.

"Yes, that's what I want, too," agreed Gilda.

"Let's get some lunch," said Dad. "We've got a lot of catching up to do."

Made in the USA
Lexington, KY
15 September 2012